William Allingham

Thought and Word and Ashby Manor

A Play in Two Acts

William Allingham

Thought and Word and Ashby Manor
A Play in Two Acts

ISBN/EAN: 9783337397623

Printed in Europe, USA, Canada, Australia, Japan

Cover: Foto ©Andreas Hilbeck / pixelio.de

More available books at **www.hansebooks.com**

AND

Ashby Manor

A PLAY IN TWO ACTS

BY

WILLIAM ALLINGHAM

WITH PORTRAIT
FOUR DESIGNS FOR STAGE SCENES BY MRS. ALLINGHAM
AND
A SONG WITH MUSIC

LONDON
REEVES AND TURNER, 196 STRAND
1890

TO MY CHILDREN,

HOPING THEY (IF NO OTHERS) WILL BRING
A SYMPATHETIC ATTENTION TO THESE ENDEAVOURS
TO PUT IN WORDS
SOME FAINT HINT OF THE HIGHEST TRUTHS
INEXPRESSIBLE IN ANY FORM OF LANGUAGE.

CONTENTS.

———•◦•———

ON A PORTRAIT.

When a Poet knew himself, once on a time,
And his joy of life overflow'd into rhyme,
He had supple joints and curly dark hair;
Folk see him now with a pate half bare,
Some grizzled locks hanging lichen-wise
Over wrinkled forehead and sunken eyes:
But why not show him (guarding truth)
As he used to be in his days of youth?
Look and believe! he once was young;
When he sung of Love, he felt what he sung;
A Poet then, if a Poet now,
Why with sad cheer and wither'd brow
Greet the good Friend who may wish to learn
How he look'd?—He looked *thus*, on the Banks of
    Erne,
(Nay, younger still, and merrier far,—
Already long set is the morning star)
Erne water dancing from dawn to dark:
Over the green hills caroll'd the lark,
Seagull screech'd over ocean-strand,
Plover wail'd on the brown moorland;
Woman was loveliness; life was wide,
Fill'd with wonders on every side;
Heaven clear open as far as GOD,
Maker and Guardian of sun and clod;
Truth, unselfishness, merely were right
Poets walk'd in celestial light.
Gloom and fear and longing and pain—
He forgets them now,—is almost fain
(But no!) to wish himself young again.

HEAVEN'S GATE.

1.—2

HEAVEN'S GATE.

"THE LETTER KILLETH, BUT THE SPIRIT GIVETH LIFE."

I.

RESPECT thine office; fear no man;
Thou, Poet, art a sacristan,
(For higher creatures than poor we,
I think, are priests invisibly)
'Tis thine to tread on holy ground,
Where meaner foot is wrongly found;
'Tis thine to guard the mysteries,—
Which are not shown to mortal eyes
The purest, clearest,—from disgrace
Of idols in the sacred place.

II.

By names of Venus and of Mars
The Tuscan Exile fill'd the stars
With lover and with warrior souls:
Aloof each mighty planet rolls,
By sagest Poet unconceived.
Fancy on fancy, half-believed,
Forget how they have sprung from nought.
I often pictured in my thought
A Gate, whereof we speak and write;
And found the same at dead of night,
Neither by moon nor lantern-light.

III.

It was, in dreaming truth, a Gate
Vaster than kings go through in state,
And pierced a black gigantic wall
Immeasurably built.   To all,
Wide, without bar or valve, it stood.
And round it throng'd a Multitude,
From every nation that has birth
Between the snowy poles of Earth.

IV.

As bursts the sunshine from a cave
Of high cloud, over field and wave,
One, like a man, but more than mortal,
Radiantly issues from the Portal,—
Realm within it softly bright,
Purple shadow and golden light
On mystic mountains, happy vales,
Where circle beyond circle fails.

V.

"Come in!"—'twas music trumpet-clear,
"The Gate of Heaven is open here."
Whereat, a wind of joy and fear
Swept all that mighty Multitude
Like some great cornfield where they stood;
But only woke a whispering stress
Born from the hush of earnestness.

VI.

Then jangling tones broke up the charm,
As bells a sleeping town alarm;
"Beloved Sheep, beware, beware!
"This is no true thing, but a snare;
"We see no mark or sign or token
"Whereof the oracles have spoken.

"This like our promised Heav'n!—to mix
"With heathens and with heretics!
"Apollyon seemeth Son of Light.
"But soon the Bridegroom shall invite,
"We're saved, the others flung to Hell,
"And hallelujah! all is well.
"Close eye and ear, my brethren,—say
"Phantom! Delusion! Fiend! away!"

VII.

Suddenly a little Child
Ran up to where that Angel smiled,
And caught his skirt; who, stooping low
Lifted him; and I saw them go,
And sigh'd,—and sighing, waken'd so;
Amidst, methought, a boundless flow
Of people, many voices blent,
Sea-like; I knew not what it meant.

VIII.

Saint Wilbrod, where a Pagan King
Knelt at the font, had bow'd to fling
Miraculous water on his head;
But the grave King rose up, and said,
"This was not thought of; can'st thou tell
"If my forefathers be in Hell,
"Or Heaven?" "In Hell," the Saint's reply:
To whom the King with loftier eye,
"Enough! I will not quit my race."
—To answer, *Heaven is not a place,*
Were bringing passports to disgrace.

IX.

Such doctrines Mather fear'd at Salem,
And, lest his own belief should fail him,
(So godly, that he turn'd inhuman)
Hang'd twice a week some poor old woman;

Nay, Brother Burroughs' self, who doubted,—
That Scripture's letter be not scouted;
Which, with all marvels big and little,
Not held and hugg'd in every tittle,
Faith were slain dead (that's now so strong),
And Truth, and Sense of Right and Wrong;
Yes, the ALMIGHTY then, no doubt,
From soul of man were blotted out.

X.

Predominancy, a great tree
Of Upas kind, drips constantly
The violent poison, Persecution;
Greater the marvel, tho', if you shun
Harm from a small infesting weed
Which doth the self-same venom breed,
Verbality, whose mesh is found
In every field and garden-ground.
Spirit to spirit, we are wise
To meditate of mysteries,
To see a little, dark and dim,
For mortals are not Seraphim.

XI.

A Dream should as a Dream be told,
Nor do I this of mine uphold
Above the dreams of other men,
Where all is out of waking ken.
Let's to our daylight tasks and trust
The future, as we ought and must.
Go, noisy tongues, howe'er you will!
One hath His plan, who keepeth still.
What is, He sees,—we cannot see;
He knows, we know not, what shall be.

XII.

Tho' High-Priest, Medicine-man, nor Lama,
Zerdusht, Mohammed, Buddha, Brahma,

Nor any Teacher, mild or blatant,
For true Religion hold a patent,
Can mathematicise the line
Connecting Human and Divine,
The line, say rather, that doth reach
From GOD to every soul and each,—
Tho' every parable and vision
Of scenes infernal and elysian,
By prophet-poet's genius told,
Re-echo'd thousand-million-fold,
Whether of Greek, or Jew, or Swede,
Be rich poetic truth indeed,
No legal document to read,—
Tho' man's best wisdom on the earth,
Man's learning, be as little worth
For this, as to be six feet one
Helps you to pry into the sun,—
Still, when the Soul is walking right,
HEAVEN is sure to come in sight,
Near or distant, faint or bright.

LEVAVI OCULOS.

IN trouble for my sin, I cried to God;
    To the Great God who dwelleth in the deeps.
The deeps return not any voice or sign.

But with my soul I know thee, O Great God;
The soul thou gavest knoweth thee, Great God;
And with my soul I sorrow for my sin.

Full sure I am there is no joy in sin,
Joy-scented Peace is trampled under foot,
Like a white growing blossom into mud.

Sin is establish'd subtly in the heart
As a disease; like a magician foul
Ruleth the better thoughts against their will.

Only the rays of God can cure the heart,
Purge it of evil: there's no other way
Except to turn with the whole heart to God.

In heavenly sunlight live no shades of fear;
The soul there, busy or at rest, hath peace;
And music floweth from the various world.

The Power is great and good, and is our God.
There needeth not a word but only these;
Our God is good, our God is great.   'Tis well.

All things are ever God's; men's thoughts of things
Are warp'd with evil will and stain'd with sin;
God, and the things of God, immutable.

Great Master, how I fain would lift myself
Above men's network foolishness, and move
In thy unfenced, unmeasured warmth and light!

Lo, when I rise a very little way,
The fences, nets, and pitfalls change to lines
Drawn on a map; anon they disappear;

All shows of things are seen as parts of truth
My soul, if busy or at rest, hath peace,
Hath visions of the House of Perfect Peace!

PHANTOM DUTY.

SLOW-BURNING in the cavern's depth appears
 The Talismanic Lamp which rules the spheres
Of men and spirits. Safely he hath pass'd
Swords, flames, ghouls, dragons, demons; but at last
A Phantom, like his Mother, sadly stands
Full in the destined way, with warning hands.
He pauses, he forgets, he sinks, he sleeps :
And in Elysium his true Mother weeps.

SUNDAY BELLS.

SWEET Sunday Bells! your measured sound
   Enhances that repose profound
Of all the golden fields around,
And range of mountain, sunshine-drown'd.

Amid the cluster'd roofs outswells,
And wanders up the winding dells,
And near and far its message tells,
Your holy song, sweet Sunday Bells!

Sweet Sunday Bells! ye summon round
The youthful and the hoary-crown'd,
To one observance gravely bound;
Where comfort, strength, and joy are found.

The while, your cadenced voice excels
To waken memory's tender spells;
Revives old joy-bells, funeral-knells,
And childhood's far-off Sunday Bells.

O Sunday Bells! your pleading sound
The shady spring of tears hath found,
In one whom neither pew nor mound
May harbour in the hallow'd ground:

Whose heart to your old music swells:
Whose soul a deeper thought compels;
Who like an alien sadly dwells
Within your chime, sweet Sunday Bells!

SEE what lives of mortals are
  On our foolish little star!
Toil unceasing, pleasure flying,
Aspiration fall'n to sighing,
Old deceits in garbs newfangled,
Angel-wings with cobwebs tangled,
Selfish comfort, drugg'd with sense,
Ambition's poverty immense,
Tender memory, sad in vain,
Flickering hope and haunting pain,
Cries of suffering, sweat of strife,—
But where the strong victorious life?
    Perchance its deeds make little noise;
No record of its pains and joys,
Save in mystic forms enscroll'd,
Spiritual eyes behold,
Seeing what lives of mortals are
On our foolish little star.

AN EVIL MAY-DAY.

In the Soul's sky may dawn an Evil Day,
First of a Time of Horror and Dismay,
Which only GOD's own sun can chase away.

AN EVIL MAY-DAY.

PART I.

SUDDENLY, softly, I awoke from sleep;
My lattice open to the morning sun,
Call of a distant cuckoo, lyric notes
Of many a voice, leaf-whispers.
      May, once more,
Her dewy fragrant kiss, and all the love
It wakes us to,—a joyous, beauteous world!
Long shadows lying on the luminous grass;
The lilac's purple honeycombs enswathed
In freshest foliage; snowy pear-tree bloom;
Birds on our daisied lawn, or flitting swift
Through floating under-boughs to elmtops fledged
Against the tenderly translucent sky;
And, through the leafage, glimpses of a realm
Of woodland slopes and vales, and distant hills
Of bright horizon. O the sweet old rapture!
May in my inmost soul awaking too.
This might be Earth's first morning, or the rise
Of that New Heav'n and Earth—
      Ah pain! ah grief!
As happy wingèd thing afloat on air
Smit with a cruel pang, down-fluttering, drops,
My heart so fell—
    They say "There is No God!"

Evil May-day, by my account. Long since,
Whispers of bale were rife; dark prophecies
And dim forebodings brought a passing qualm,
A momentary shiver; that was all:

2

As peradventure may a man have heard
Rumour of pestilence in Eastern lands,
Of little import: "creeping westward" next:
"Within our country's border" (this is grave):
And then a pause, time slides, the man has turn'd
To his affairs and pleasures; when one day
What's this the mirror shows him?—Heaven and
    Hell!
The plague-spot on his tongue!   His lot is drawn.

Yes, look upon thy hands and touch thy head;
'Tis thou—that wakedst oft in other Mays,
Didst kneeling say thy pray'r, and look aloft
As into thy dear Father's face, and see
His handiwork all round thee, all done right:
The lilies of the field and the seven stars,
Beast, bird, and insect, and immortal Man.
"These are Thy glorious works, Parent of good!"—
"In wisdom hast Thou made them all."
                            Poor fool!
Gaze round upon the flow'rs and grass and sunshine,
Bathe in their brightness, hear the senseless birds
Chatter and chirp, and be thou merry too.
All's but a dream; and why torment thyself?
—Because the plague is come.   The bird is hit.
The dream is *fled;* and now I wake aghast.
I see this world a body without soul;
I see the flow'rs and greenery of May
A garland on a corpse.   "There is No God."

Nay, courage! let the fearful mood pass by.
Here is no plague.   Behind those branching elms
Our shady lane winds to the village green,
Its ancient cottages, its ivied tower,
With graves of twenty generations.   Hark!
The dial: sturdy Labour forth has trudged
With tools in hand; Age on his doorstep greets

The friendly radiance ; Childhood swarms to school
And hums like bees in clover, till the song
Heartily rises ; and our week moves round,
As weeks and years and centuries have moved,
Over this English village in its vale,
Secluded from the world,—not separate.
There goes the flutter of a distant train
Speeding to the great city full of men
And men's accumulated thought and work,
With ships from every sea along her wharves.
Art thou delirious ? or wilt thou count
All this, insanity—the varied life
In fields and cities, work and worship and love,
Whate'er binds men together, linking past,
Present, and future—
     O let be ! let be !
No form of speech can do me any good,
My own or other men's devisal, fresh
As primrose, venerable as churchyard yew.
Having heard sentence pass'd, no other words
Can carry meaning ; one brief dismal phrase
Knolls on the air—" No God ! " and still—" No God ! "

 Pretence of continuity ! talk, preach,
Write books ; build cities, churches, monuments ;
Patch up and varnish histories, pedigrees ;
Take childish titles, worship toyshop crowns ;
Sustain (save when alone or with a friend)
The masquerade of dignity ; pass on
Old phrases, teach them to the children ; make
Your little mark, or big, as one who scribes
Two letters, or full name, or date therewith,
Upon a tree, and dies, and in a while
The tree perishes also. Vain conceit !
Swim with me, fellow-bubbles, catch fine hues
And picture-like reflections, and then burst !
The swift stream flows, the shoreless sea of forms

Melting, reshaping, seeming (since our life
Is like a flash of lightning) permanent;
But rolling ever from darkness into darkness.
God was behind that darkness once;—that sea
His effluent power.   But now, there is No God.

After the first sharp pain I wrote this down
To ease awhile my heart-ache.   Count not these
But idle words; for since I wotted first
Of my own being, never grief like that.
"Able to soothe all sadness but despair"
The poet sang: no finest solaces
Had any comfort.   Through the dismal time
I dragg'd from sleep to sleep, groaning the while,
As one sore-wounded drags from pause to pause;
And sleep was like a swoon, or else perturb'd
With shapeless terror.

                      But sleep grew more calm
(I know not when or how began the change)—
And all things with it: wind and wave went down,
And life took on its ordinary look
By slow gradations.   All was as before?
Not so.   I was not in perpetual pain;
Only half-paralysed.   Month after month,
And after that sad year, another year,
And after this, another year: I went
And came and talk'd and laugh'd, like those around
      me:
Only I recollected now and then,
And shiver'd, whispering to myself "No God."

No God, No Soul; they are the self-same thought.
And I, that think it, turning into mire
To-morrow or next year, I care not much
What may befall a race of things like me,
A little better luck, a little worse,
As each flits by and vanishes for ever.

To-morrow will be Nothing; and To-day
That leads to it, is Next to Nothing. Go!
Laugh, weep, do what you will, eat, drink, and die—
The sad old phrase found true.
                              Is't selfishness
Thus craves for God, that God may give us life
After this life? New life be as it may.
That irks me nothing. It is this my life
I would not lose, the life within this life.
And I have lost it, if there be No God.

———

Part II.

OF all pathetic things the most is this—
       A happy bright-eyed Child, some four years old,
Making acquaintance with man's common world.
Joy, wonder, eager questionings; anon
An anxious look, a swift and wide-eyed stare
At his dear Oracle; and merry laughs
And low contented songs made by himself
Are his; and youthful strange imaginings!
And sometimes you may see those innocent eyes
Fix'd in a meditative trance, the while
He strives to see some vaguest vapoury form
Of thought within him.
                              O this world of ours!

I am your Prophet, Priest, and Oracle,
My little Son; whatever I respond
Is fate. One only answer vexes you—
"I do not know." You try and try again
For something better, and are ill-content.
But often must you hear those baffling words;

And often must you say them to yourself
When manhood, which you deem omniscient,
Is yours in turn,—is like what we have found.
O guard thee, Prophet, well, not to mislead
Thy neophyte! The dream, the phantasy
Thou puttest in his mind, is truth for him,
Until he finds it untrue. This young soul
Tremulous with wonder, curiosity,
Imagination, (look but in his face)
Drinks in the world through every joyful sense;
Sensation turns to thought and thought revives
Sensation in the memory; thus is built
The body of the mind by slow degrees,
With order'd imagery, with habitudes
Of movement; and the little world it lives in
Is its own making chiefly. All the while,
The great world lives around it, and includes
It with the rest of things. A word of mine,
Be it the emptiest breath, can take firm shape
In my son's world; the herald's animals,
Insert them in his natural-history book,
Were just as credible as any there;
Angel is no whit harder to conceive
Than eagle, and a Heaven above the clouds
(Reach'd by balloon perhaps) much easier
Than suns and planets and space without a bound.
  Thou shalt not build a false world, little Son,
If skill of mine can sift the follies out
Men have mix'd up with everything. My care
Is less to teach than save thee from being taught
Half-truths and falsehoods in thy tender time.

  Beware, my Son, of words! The Human Race
Hath stored its wisdom there, its errors there,
Mistakes and follies and duplicities.
Of words false gods are made, each doom'd at last
A worn-out idol to the lumber-loft

Or trim museum,—concourse wonderful,
Superb, grotesque, pathetic, and obscene!

 Childhood will ask, " Who made all these things ? "
  " God."
" Where does God live ? "—suppose I point and say,
" On that high mountain top"; my child regards
The peak with joyful awe; but one day climbs
And finds a barren frosty crag,—nor heeds
The wide spread glory of things encircling it.
He hears of Heaven above the clouds; his book
At school confutes it : starry heaven goes blank.
Words said to children can be only true,
Or not, in their direct and simple sense.
" At such and such a place, God walked with men ;
They saw and heard Him ; what he said and did
Is warrant for your duties and your hopes."
The warm young spirit trustfully accepts,
Lies down, uprises, in a full belief,
From day to day, for many days and years,
Till one day comes the question, " Is this true ? "
Nay, teach the plans, ways, character of God,
With Man's relations to Him thence deduced,
In any form of words you will : how fence
The fatal question out—" But is this true ? "
The answer " No ! " smites all truth to the ground,
The vine and prop together ; Truth itself,
Immortal Truth, lies murder'd !
     Foolishness,
Dishonesty and cowardice of men,
What bitter pain, what cruel wrongs ye breed !
As if our case were not perplex'd enough,
And troublesome enough, and sad enough,
But we must writhe in self-inflicted pangs !

 But in the reign of Science you are born.
Theology, with pomp and riches yet,

Sits mumbling, droning, in his padded chair,
Gouty, asthmatic, ailing every way.
A young audacious voice rings through the land—
" Ask questions, men, where ye may hope reply
By gauge of human faculties, may test
Reply when found.   First cause and final cause
In every case being out of reach, henceforth
Fix eye and thought upon the scrutable ;
Travel, examine, and subdue throughout
The great domain of Science ; step by step,
Link after link, trace, test, confirm and fix
The sequences of natural law ; reduce
The complex to the simple ; thus control,
So far as man may do so, human life,
The race itself ; attain, whate'er it be,
No twilight Land of Dreams, Fool's Paradise
Hid in a theologic labyrinth
Or metaphysic jungle.   How sublime
In its simplicity, one single fact
In pure mechanic formula express'd,
(Shall it be call'd *Vibration?*—possibly)
And all phenomena its aspects merely !
This we shall find at last."

> And then? what then
Are we at home henceforward in the world?
All comfortably settled in our minds,
Knowing the immortal truth—Vibration?
Shall we spoonfeed our babes on science-pap,
Till teeth find tougher work? train them to scan
The mechanism of all phenomena,
To measure and set it down in proper form,—
The *ne plus ultra* this, which cannot baulk?
  Again I say, Beware of words, my Son.
Exact and systematic knowledge—good !
But now, of what?   Of the true nature of things?
That is abjured.   No step found possible
In that direction.   Of phenomena?

"Surely." But I deny it: very close
We peer, and make our atoms very small,
Yet after all 'tis but the coarser part
Of any one phenomenon of nature
Which we can measure and make record of.
Science is measurement, no more, no less,
Whatever sauce we add. Minds wholly fill'd
With Physical Science (and a fond conceit
That they alone know Nature) miss and lose
The natural appearances of things
Beyond all common ignorance. Day and night,
Earth, ocean, sky, the seasons, peopled full
With countless forms of life ; a world imbued
With mystic beauty, wonder, awfulness,
Powers inexpressible and infinite,
Whereto man's spirit exquisitely thrills,
Raised, rapt, and soaring on celestial wings,—
Which ecstasy begetteth Art in some,
In every sane soul Worship in some wise,
Voiceful or silent,—shall we see instead
The tall ghost of a pair of compasses
Stalking about a world of diagrams,
And algebraic regiments that march
And countermarch, and wheel?

          O learn all this —
If so thou fail not to come back at last,
My son, to nature's own rich symbolism !
Value *appearances*, and study these
To see them well,—your first relationship,
Your last and truest too, with circumstance ;
More excellent by far to apprehend
Than all disclosures of analysis.
Upon the surface earthly Beauty blooms,
Yielding itself to every loving eye,
Known heavenly in its correspondences
When Seer or Poet comes ; immortal flow'r,
Belovèd of Man's soul, no trivial thing,

No fleeting thing as flimsy proverbs wail!
Inferior truths are good in their degree,
But the first-met is first, nor ever can
Be weigh'd or measured.   That the world is fair
Concerns us more than that the world is round,
(Though this, like every truth, be well to fix);
The rose, the primrose, and the hawthorn-flow'r.
The colours of the dawn or evening air,
Clouds, mountains, rivers, woodlands, grassy meads,
The varying ocean and the starry night,
The countless shapes of animals, and most
The human form, and miracle of face,
Have in their beauty more significance
Than tabulated light-waves which impinge
On optic nerves and yield the brain a sense
Of red, blue, yellow—Science knows not how.
Science can but afford a pitying smile
If you forget that just where warmth begins
Of human interest in a question, there
Science stops short.   And let her have the praise
Of keeping in her limit, if she keep,
And lack not limitation's humbleness.

Beware, I say, of words, warm, wide, and loose;
Beware of cold and rigid formulæ
No less; both full of power—they are not things,
Nor even thoughts, but shadowings-forth of thoughts,
Wearing a phantom dignity themselves.
True, that we think by these: most men by words,
The grave mathematician by his signs,
Expressing a mechanic universe,
Yet giving irrepressible Fancy room
To sport in magical curves and deem herself
Almost creative in mechanic wise,
Leaving out life and beauty merely.   Words
Have melody and colour, and therewith
The Poet's art can build a lovelier world,

Nay, truer than the common, for the gold
Is smelted from the dross that made it dull.
Be ever thankful of poetic truth,
And hold it fast. Value *Appearances*,
And let *Imagination* teach their worth,
Counting this practical. A sane clear mind
To see, and to imagine, is a mind
Of noblest rank : learning will nourish it,
But not to any show of learning : such
Are Seers and Poets. Through appearances
Beheld with keen and sympathetic eyes
Imaginative insight pierces deep
To something secret,—not mechanical
But spiritual, and wholly beyond reach
Of Science, which too often is so vain
As therefore to deny it scornfully ;
Spiritual, and not contain'd or circumscribed
In any science ever formulated,
Or any creed that is or will be made,
Or aught that eye can see, or ear can hear ;
For subtler, dearer, more delicious beauty
Lives in the soul than in the outer world,
And therefore fact is poor to dreams and hopes,
Child-fancies beggar all the famous things.
　Ah, might we trust the Poets all in all !
Too often they divert themselves and us
With gambols in the air. Amorous of words,
Temptable by a rhyme or phrase, they make
Language their end not means ; or sometimes stoop
To stroke the public ear and give those jaws
The food they gape for.
　　　　　　Men, in short, my Son,
Speak truth by most imperfect signs at best,
And with it many follies, many lies,
Deceiving or deceived, being only men,
Weak, wavering, limited. Yet men alone
See, note, explore, make record of, would fain,

But cannot ever, comprehend the world,
Life being a mystery, not a mechanism;
Orderly Miracle, where some men see
The Order, some the Wonder, most, and shape
Their diagrams, their phantasies; the Wise,
Wedding experience and imagination—
Both; and lift up their eyes and hands to God.

As to the Future, that is God's affair.
I am not Ruler of the Universe,
Nor in His secrets; but I hold Him good,
His riches boundless, and His will to give.
Also that Man has share, whatever share,
In working out the Universal Plans,
And man's own fate is partly in his power
For each of us; how far we cannot know.
This I do know, immortal thoughts alone,
Eternal things, have interest for my soul—
That which is truly me, my inmost self.

Man can help men, and also hinder them.
Men's evil and folly are to guard against,
Assuming many shapes; not dangerous least
In Books, pretended utterances of thought.
I say it who have loved books all my life.
The tongue may lie, or, self-deceiving, show
Folly as wisdom, may omit or add,
Transpose, misrepresent: more easily
The pen; and lo, by typographic art
What inky robes of grave authority
Do words put on, and in the library
The volume takes its seat among its peers,
Or quasi-peers. Nowhere such solemn shams
As pen and printer's ink can make! Man's tongue
Is flexible, but eye, face, voice, and gesture,
Body and whole demeanour help you well
To check or to corroborate his speech
(Put faith in physiognomy!); a Book

Wears deep disguise ; may be a puppet-thing,
And not a man at all.   The World of Books
Is full of glamour ; evil, good, false, true,
Living and dead ; enchanted wilderness
Where many wander, few can find a path,
Or gather what is good for them.   My Boy,
I vow, shall not begin to read too soon !
Learning can nourish Wisdom, when good food
Is quietly digested ; but, too oft,
Unfit, ill-cook'd, or overloaded meals
Lie crude and swell the belly with wind, or breed
Dull fat, mistook for portliness and strength.
And surely never since the world began
So many Learned Fools as now-a-days,
Or Learned Folly with so loud a voice.
Even the Wiser slip from sanity
At times, and swell the roaring storm of words.

I am your Oracle and Prophet now,
Young Mortal, weak and ignorant as I am
And fain to question rather than reply.
Yet have I journey'd on the road of life
Full many a mile, and bought experiences,
Have seen, done, joy'd and suffer'd, with a soul
Not timid, neither hard, sincere in grain,
Open to every influence, not engross'd
Of any, wishing well to all I met.
On foot, but not a beggar, have I fared,
Rested in huts and inns and palace halls,
Conversed on equal terms with many men,
Crept through dark valleys, climbed the mountain tops
And known all kinds of weather.   Here I sit
By fireside, with a baby on my knee.
A Boy with golden curls and grave blue eyes.
Asking me questions.   Shall I tell him truth ?
Yes, Dearest, now and ever !   But to know
The needful questions is to be mature.

A child but asks as prompted—mostly, too,
Prompted by Ignorance in Wisdom's mask;
She uses words unmeaningly, and crowds
Life's pathways with memorials of man's folly.
Prompt him I must, and honestly give answer.
"Who made the world?"—GREAT GOD: we use that
    name.
How do we know Him?—In the heart and soul.
What is He?—No man hath the power to know."
This is enough to tell him at the time.

    Man hath no thoughts to think what GOD is like,
And much less words to say; but he can feel
At times the Presence great and wonderful
Beyond all words and thoughts and dreams, and yet
Wherein we live and move and have our being.
All great truths are incomprehensible;
Much more the Living Centre of them all.
The clearest moments of the noblest men
Give insight thitherward, and what they see
Belongs to man, though some regard it not.
Soon the clouds roll together, the ground-fogs
Grow thick, and all the vision disappears;
But what the best eyes at their best behold
Is Truth Divine; the test whereof is this—
A lofty sanity of thought and life
In whoso doth receive it, harmony
Felt in his inmost being, nor wholly hid
From other men. But how impossible
To put the vision into words, nor weave
Therewith a snare! O folly, to suppose
That speech, however wonderful it be,
Is more than makeshift! Could I stop thine ears
Till thou art somewhat ripened in thy mind,
My Son, from all more free discourse of God,
Dogmatic, controversial, personal,
I would; and I will do it, all I can.

It may be thou art born to a troublous time,
Retributive on nations for their sins.
At least, thou shalt escape one evil thing—
My Evil May-day, doleful to endure,
Sad to remember.   Yet it pass'd; I live;
And God lives.

PART III.

AND God lives.   Yes, begin and end with that,
  For, whichsoever way you turn your face
And journey through th' illimitable vast,
You come to Nothing or you come to God.
   "We come to Matter," you reply, "more Matter,
Matter in many forms, ourselves being of them,
Man too is made of world-stuff."
                        Which contains
No mind, affection, moral principle,
Or ruling will; yet breeds them in its dance
Of purposeless gyration, turns (O strange!)
At last to speculation on itself,
And finds at choice, dust or divinity.
—I say, we come to Nothing, or to God.
   'Confront us then with Him.   Who sees his face
Or hears his voice?   They told us in our youth
He paced a garden, spoke from a certain hill,
And wore a man's true body for a time.
They painted Him, an Old Man propt on clouds,
A Young Man, flowing-hair'd, with aureole,
Walking on water, flying through the air;
Much wondrous, much familiar circumstance.
But all this fading into fairy-tales,
What have we?'

        Truth.   And know this well, once more,
Every high truth is inexpressible,
And God, the highest, absolutely.   Men
Strive after some conception, symbol-wise,
But make, too often, symbol into idol;
And all these idols forged by human brain,
Better or worse, and aiding more or less,
Misleading less or more, long-lived or short,
Are perishable things. The idol falls;
And then it seems the pillars of the world
That break, the roof of heav'n that crashes in.
A little cloud of dust was in our eyes;
Look up: God sits enthroned, thy lord and king;
Look round, His earth is wide and beautiful.
If once thou hast that vision, treasure it,
Speak little of it, let it nourish thy life
In fair thoughts, just deeds, and self-harmony,
While the unceasing noise of human talk
Hums round unheeded, and the multitude
Concerns itself with whatsoe'er it will.
Jove's thunderbolt, Apollo's fiery car,
Being phrases put aside, seems solar force
Less wonderful, or th' all-pervasive thrill
Of electricity? The human mind
And moral laws, do these depend on names?
The world is wider, deeper than our thought;
We walk as if in twilight: but, at times,
How, whence, we know not, all is lighted up,
Transfigured. What is shown to us? A glimpse
Of inmost truth.
            So and not otherwise
Poetic and religious thoughts are born,
Nor else interpretable. This great Light,
More glorious than the sun's, this Divine Stream
This emanation from the Life of Life,
Named or not named, and fitliest received
With silent joy, these cloudless blissful hours

Or moments, who shall hope to represent?
The finest mesh of words being all too coarse,
The loftiest tones of poem or of creed
But distant echoes of the vibrant Soul
Throbbing and pulsing in its bath of Light,
Fill'd with the presence of the Living God,
One Power evolving multiformity,
Pervading and transcending every form.
　　Such vision you may keep, or you may lose.
And what destroys it, or prevents it? This—
The setting-up False Vision in its place,
By obsolete pretended evidence,
Untrue in fact, impossible in kind,
Still palm'd on innocent souls when full of trust
And love and wonder. Once these holy names
And emblems meant what now they cannot mean,
As well thou knowest; yet thou teachest them
For absolute truth to tender longing souls,
Fastening their faith, their highest faculty,
To forms decay'd, worm-eaten through and through.
Vile coward! murderer of thy children's peace,
Preparing for them sick and crooked lives,
The end perhaps despair. But God's light shines,
Though men shut out, discolour, distort the ray.
　　Man, in a sense, makes God. In the same sense
Man makes the world: his world is what he makes it
Each man his world, his God. But tell me now:
The natural, true, and most miraculous World,
Which no man ever saw, can ever see,
The Living Absolute Eternal God,
Whom no man ever saw, can ever see,—
Do these depend on how a man shall think
Or picture them, or any set of men?
The God a man hath made he may pull down
The World a man makes alters with himself
The true, the everlasting Life remains,
Surest of all things,—personal, universal,

Ineffable, incomprehensible,
Perceived, received, as with the flower of the soul.
God rules us whether we take heed or no.
'Tis duty less than privilege and joy
To recognise Him ; nor such boon to all
In equal measure.   Judge its potency
In the few most receptive, not the crowd.
To live, one needs not know that earth is round,
Much less the laws of planets and of suns,
But, all men ignorant, each man were lower'd,
And crippled even in his daily needs.
Were all born blind, then who would guess the light ?
All deaf, then who imagine any sound ?
And many see the light who nothing know
Of the Sun's greatness, only dimly see
The beauty it gives birth to ; many have ears
And yet by music's magic no more touch'd
Than carven figures by the organ-storm
Shaking their substance atoms.   Must thou gain
These other men's impossible consent
Before thou tremblest to the mystic joy
That frees thy spirit with a gift of wings
In Music's atmosphere ? or give account
To them of how and why thou thus art moved
By Beauty, natural or interpreted ?
Doubt, or distrust, or disbelieve, since some
With ears that hear not, eyes that cannot see,
Bring scales to measure and weigh your consciousness ?
Nay, know'st thou Love ?—a Love sublime and pure,
The world's transfiguration, through thy soul's.
If thou hast ever been assured of this,
Shall icy hearts or sneering tongues convict
High Love, and not themselves, of foolishness ?
Consider then : if that most glorious Power
Far beyond audible and visual sense,
Felt at the inmost of thy soul of souls
In moments clear and rare, at other times

Be thickly veil'd from thee or quite obscured,
Wilt thou accept the bright hour or the dark
To teach thee truth? If certain other men
Deny the vision wholly, wilt thou choose
Negation for thy having? and because
Of the great glory and wonder of the light
That shone upon thee, say it was a dream,
No truth at all? Forget Him if thou wilt.
Deny Him. Thou art free. Nor will He strike
With angry flash; not so the world is made.
No penalties are set for unbelief,
Except the natural and inevitable
Contain'd in not believing. Count these nothing,—
Who shall refute, gainsay thee? go thy ways;
The loss is in thyself; and if unfelt,
The greater. Even as the man devoid
Of music misses nothing, loveless man
Pines not for lack of love, so he to whom
This world is empty of Divinity
From earth's dark centre to the Milky Way,
Sees this world full as other men's, and seems
To live in the same world. O marvellous!
Here walk two human creatures side by side:
But seest thou in what kind of world each moves?
Not with the bodily eye. Each makes his world,
And counts his own the only. To but few
Is given the Poet's, Prophet's ecstasy:
Yet theirs the witness we accept at last.

Many are dull and scarcely heed at all.
But some turn all to question :—" What is Life,
This marvel of all marvels? Show to us
Without delay, Whence, How, and What it is,
Or must we not affirm it meaningless?
At most, a puzzle fit to stretch our wits,
The whilst we eat, drink, fight, laugh, propagate,
And play at reason, virtue, and so forth?

Guess it a dustheap, somehow grown alive,
Or else a sort of mental phantasy?
Surely, if we can't sift things, we have right
To rate them as we choose."   There wisdom spoke!
Not peevish folly, or forward babyhood.
But this at least is true beyond a doubt,—
Man's Life *has* meaning, else the World has none,
This Universe is but a puff of smoke
Floating in whirls about the gulf of space,
We atoms in the midst, and all our thoughts
Are less than nothing.
       What Life is, I know not,
Nor claim the right to know; but gladly accept
The highest hints and intimations given,
As likest truth.   I know not what God is,
Nor count it reasonable to suppose
A man could know; but that God lives and rules,
My soul in times of pure and tranquil vision
Sees without effort; which great central truth
Sways into order all the world of thought,
That else were chaos.   And, since I am I,
To me, a person, He, a person, lives;
A Living God, of power immeasurable,
Nature incomprehensible, and plans
Inscrutable; of whom I know by faith,—
A reasonable and necessary faith,
Correlative to ignorance, and yet
No way self-contradictory, a clue
In a prodigious labyrinth, a lamp
In a great darkness.

       Why no more is known?
Enough it is the nature of things; and how
In sooth could I conceive it otherwise,
Create a different world?   What use this faith?—
What use wide-sweeping universal thoughts?
Nay what use is the Universe itself? . . .

At least we'll take for granted it exists,
Though questions may lack answers! "Matter,"
   "Spirit,"
What may these be? one thing, or separate?—
I care not which; for how should that concern?
All is, of need, connected, up and down,
And grossest link'd with subtlest. We must live
In a material world, must therein work,
Thereby be wrought upon. I am conjoin'd—
This personal I, (invisible as God)—
To my own bodily organs first of all;
Related strictly to the beast, the bird,
The blade of grass, the clod of earth, the cloud,
The faintest haze of suns within the sky.
That nearest fiery orb makes flow my blood;
Electric ether vivifies my brain;
And I, made up of these, who am not these,
Exist in personal being, think, enquire,
Reason, imagine, feel, and nothing know:
But in my dearest moments I think—God.
Ask you, What use is Faith? Faith is like Health:
Which, if you have in full serene possession,
You feel it every moment of the day,
In every fibre of your frame, each mood
And movement of your mind, yet for most part
Unconsciously. Inherit health and lose it,
Then shall you know its worth. But some poor men
Have never had it, and their seeming life
Is three parts death; some fling away their share
To buy diseases, or, when sense is dull'd,
Count dulness armour, take defect for strength;
Few have full measure: O to be like them!
For health is life, tho' sickness in a sort
Lives on, and nearly all the world is sick.
Faith is a higher wider subtler health,
What ether is to air, what harmony
Is to a throng of disconnected sounds;

A pure truth inexpressible in words,
All the great truths being measureless, and God
The truth of truths.

      Spend not thy life in questions :
Go on thy journey, find there what thou may'st.
The past is past and had its own beliefs,
To day lies round, pours in, miraculous,
And in man's soul the springs of prophecy
Well up from their unfathomable source
Unceasingly, while he has faith in God.
Belief in God—here is the fountain-head
Of all religion, and, could that run dry
To all the human race, then human life
Were but a sandy desert full of asps.
No God—No Man.   Blind matter all without ;
Within delusive shadows.   Hold God fast.

   May-Day was evil when I miss'd my God :
Earth, sea and sky fall'n empty of a sudden.
All the wide universe a dismal waste
Peopled with phantoms of my flitting self,
And mocking gleams chance-kindled and chance
    quench'd,
All meaning nothing.   Natural May-Day
Revived to me when I found God again ;
World full of beauty and significance
Wisely and justly govern'd, and I too
Part and partaker of the wondrous whole ;
Made capable to feel, enjoy, adore,
To think and reason, not to comprehend.

Manhood is Freedom : O to use it well,
Acting upon the element where I move
According to its nature and my own,
(Obscurely folded in the germ at first,
Form'd by successive subtle acts of will)

Acting to greater purpose than appears;
Nor too much sorrowing over seeming loss
Nor anxious for security of gain,
Mild, equal-minded, fearless! To such level
Rise I in happy hour, spring-tide of soul,
Aware, without words, and beyond all words,
That God was, is, and evermore remains;
The Living Centre of this Universe,
Which is itself imagined and not seen;
Always the Centre, reach'd by various roads
From many points by many different minds.
Who move tow'rds Him, converge. Who move from
    Him
Diverge, and wander out to lonely Space,
Where they see nothing and hear nothing, save
A hollow echo of their own voice return'd
As from the Cavern of Eternal Death.
But from the Centre, Everlasting Life
Expands and pulses in perpetual waves.

    Man's property is Will; and he thereby
Can turn his face to God, change his own world;
For some things must be fix'd, and some left free.
See we not Good and Bad? upgoing lines
And down, to Best and Worst, to Heaven and Hell?
Man, as I deem, hath foretaste of them both.
But these, too, people image as they may
In gross fantastic verbal crudities,
Dark prisons, devils, tortures, pits of fire,
Unfading gardens, milk-white robes, gold harps,
A Heaven of vague "eternal happiness."
Not so it beckons me: pure health, fit work,
For Human Creatures chasten'd, purified,
Each to his best; each, clear in aim and course,
Doing his proper part with strenuous joy:
Humility and self-forgetfulness,
Low work or high, in boundless universe;

Not dull—a joyous, free, and busy Heaven,
Hope never baulk'd there, knowledge climbing on,
Wisdom expanding, love without a pain,
Sweet helpful interchange of thought and mirth;
Beauty to fill each spirit to its content;
Limitless growth: the Mystery Divine
Peacefully clear, yet still a Mystery,
The Spiritual Sun of all the Heavens;
Infinitely remote, but fully felt;
Whence radiate, and whereto in turn are drawn
All powers, all spirits,—the lowest in their turn

LOSS.

GRIEVE not much for loss of wealth,
   Loss of friends, or loss of fame,
Loss of years, or loss of health ;
   Answer, hast thou lost the shame
Whose early tremor once could flush
Thy cheek, and make thine eyes to gush,
And send thy spirit, sad and sore,
To kneel with face upon the floor,
Burden'd with consciousness of sin ?
Art thou cold and hard within,—
Sometimes looking back surprised
On thy old mood, scarce recognized,
As on a picture of thy face
In blooming childhood's transient grace ?
Then hast thou cause for grief ; and most
In seldom missing what is lost.
With the loss of Yesterday,
   Thou hast lost To-day, To-morrow,—
All thou might'st have been.   O pray,
   (If pray thou canst) for poignant sorrow !

DOGMATISM.

"THUS it is written."—Where? Oh, where?
    In the blue chart of the air?
In the sunlight? in the dark?
In the distant starry spark?
In the white scroll of the cloud?
In the waved line of the flood?
In the forms of peak or cliff,
In the rock's deep hieroglyph?
In the scribbled veins of metal?
In the tracings on the petal?
In the fire's fantastic loom?
In the fur, or scale, or plume?
In the greeting brother's glance?
In the corpse's countenance?
In men's real thoughts and ways?
Time's long track, or passing days?
In the cipher of the whole?
In the core of my own soul?
Nay!—I have sincerely sought,
But no glimpse of this thing caught

NEWS FROM PANNONIA.

———

A mighty Monarch, and a modest Man ;
Sweetest of Stoics since the world began.

NEWS FROM PANNONIA.

A.D. 180.

DRUSILLUS.   PROBUS.

Dru. HAIL, Probus !
Pro.   Hail, Drusillus !—thou in Rome !
Pale too, by Hercules ! Art sick, or wounded ?
Dru. Neither, my Probus. From Pannonia, I ;
A twelve days' journey. Now the Senate cons
My message, and I hurry to the bath.
Farewell, my friend ; I'll visit you to-morrow.
Pro. Nay, at this hour the public bath is throng'd,
And lo, my house at hand, and yours away
Beside the Vipsan Columns. Come, Drusillus,
Welcome awaits you, bath and robe and supper,
Not laid for guests, but large enough for two ;
And then, for March wind scours the dusty streets,
Home in my litter. Bravely said, old friend !
I will not ask your camp news, well content
To hear with Rome : we'll talk philosophy,
As many a night before—dispute, agree,
And taste again the likeness in unlikeness
Friendship is mix'd of.
Dru.   Thou may'st ask my news.
All Rome, indeed, will shortly ring with it.
Pro. Another victory and triumph ? Nay,
Not a defeat ? Why look you at me thus ?
Dru. Cæsar——
Pro.   Is dead ?
Dru.   He is.
Pro.   Aurelius dead !

O friend, a weighty message in two words!
So heavy hath not fall'n into mine ear
Since when, a youth, I heard men whispering
"Good Antoninus is no more!"—How long
Is that ago?—He was thy father's friend
I think, Drusillus, as Aurelius thine.

    Dru. He was.—Exactly nineteen years this month
My father was that captain of the guard
Who came to Antoninus, lying sick,
For the night's watchword, and the Emperor,
Fixing his mild majestic eyes on him,
Said, "*Equanimity.*"　At dawn of day
My father saw th' imperial face again
Pale, silent, and with eyes for ever closed.
And now his great adopted Son hath join'd
The shadowy multitude.　No Quadic spear
Dethroned him; it was fever's poison'd arrow
Flying invisible through the camp.　He shared
The legionaries' food and long fatigues,
And every chance of war.

    Pro.　　　　　　　　Thou too, Drusillus,
Or I mistake thee.　Therefore do not scorn
This amber liquor from my own hill-slope;
Thou hast sat beneath the vines there.　As thou wilt.
Himself was not more temperate.　Was his age
Twelve lustra?

    Dru.　　　　Save a year.

    Pro.　　　　　　　　Too short a life!

    Dru. Aurelius thought not so.　He ask'd my age
One day, and when I told him, "At two-score"—
He said—"a wise man knows what life is like,
And, though he lived a thousand years, would see
Old things in new masks merely.　Why not die?
I soon shall notch a third score on the stick,
Nor wish the game spun wearisomely out.
The Roman death," he said, "a free man's choice
Is rational, bold; great men have chosen it;

But I for my part rather will await
Th' appointed hour of natural release,
Patient of life, not fearing death at all ;
A sentry at his post."

    Pro.   Go on, Drusillus !

    Dru. "Why," said the Emperor, "should death
      be dreadful?
Since it is nothing but a natural change,
One other needful movement in a world
Where all things always move, and nothing stays,
Yet nothing is destroy'd. Why shrink from change
That Power which governs all things, changes all,
And makes from out their substance, other things,
From these things other yet, continually ;
And by the flow of this perpetual change
Keeps universal nature always young."

    Pro. Thy memory's good.

    Dru.   I noted down his words.
"The world, could'st thou but see it, would be seen
Shifting incessantly, but nothing lost,
And the great Whole continuing : the Gods
Also continuing, as I well believe."

    Pro. Would that we might have clearer news of
      them !
In Rome, as well thou knowest, many men
Scoff at the Gods and count them fables merely.
What would they say to this? "Assuredly
Cæsar must keep the temples up !"—or else,
"Old-fashioned ! Out of date !"

    Dru.   But here indeed
No Pontiff spoke : for one thing stay'd with him
Since Verus was his name, and Hadrian
Who loved the boy call'd him *Verissimus ;*
From youth to age, truth was his very nature,
Nor custom nor tradition master'd him,
All was digested in his mind, which took
Its proper nutriment ; nor he the fool

To think, like many, truths wear out with time—
Being more substantial than the sea and land.

   Pro. I trust his moderate and measured phrase
Beyond all flourishes.

   Dru.   He hated those.
"The Gods," he said, "we name them as we will:
They stand above my knowledge: but I feel
A Power Divine within me and without
Whereby all things are govern'd, changed, preserved."
And on another day these words were his:
" All from the Gods is full of Providence,
Nor Fortune separate from Nature ; all
Being interwoven in one mighty web.
Why therefore should I fear to quit the earth,
If this be so ? And if it be not so,
Why should I care to live in such a world,
Empty of Gods and void of Providence ?"

   Pro. Wise words !—and here no trivial theorist,
But Roman Cæsar, mightiest of men.
What will his son be like ?

   Dru.   As the Gods please.
High man or low man, wise man is the man.
Marcus himself would many a time declare,
" Great Alexander, Julius, and Pompeius,
Count I but small, if match'd with Socrates,
Or Heraclitus, or Diogenes,
Or that Greek Slave."

   Pro.   Ay, noble Epictetus.
Aurelius would have made that slave his friend.
But let us talk of Commodus awhile.
Where is he ?

   Dru.   In the camp. Aurelius turn'd
By nature to Philosophy. He said
" The senate gave me empire, not desired,
Much better loving shady silent paths
Of peaceful meditation, than to roll
On dusty highway in triumphal car.

But all things moved together to that end,
Adoption, training, much experience gain'd
In public functions, most of all the wish
Of him my more than father; and with these—
The driving-wheel of all—sense of man's place
And work, as social and for general use."

Pro. A noble nature!

Dru. Well brought-up withal.
He loved to praise his tutors—"Thanks to them
For what I am." But he was ever humble.
"I know," he said, "being prince, and train'd
        thereto,
I've miss'd much man-lore simple men have gain'd
Simply, as husbandmen grow weatherwise
And fishers wary."

Pro. There is truth in that.
Alp sees not close but wide. Nor can the great
Well know the teasing troubles of poor men.
Was he a bookish man?

Dru. His books were few.
I've heard him say, "Much reading is but vain.
In contemplation and experience
The wise man will discover what he needs,
Unmesh'd in subtleties and speculations
Thin-spun by curious busy-idle wits.
The sense of things is plain to healthy minds,
The nature of them deep beyond all ken:
Of qualities we learn; of essence nothing;
Nor do I deem, in myriad years to come,
Though many little truths they pick or delve
And put in storehouse, men are like to know
One atom more of Life, Death, or the Gods
Than we do now; nor shall they profit much
In happiness, perchance, by all they learn.
To view the daily earth and nightly heavens,
Feeling their beauty and magnificence;
To know there's good and evil, choose the good;

Let reason govern thee, not appetite ;
Learn to be true, just, diligent, and brave ;
Count all men brothers, work for general use ;
Obey God, help men, and be not perturb'd,
Taking thy lot with equanimity ;
These are the main things, and must always be ;
What more we add, not much, though we should set
The sun and moon in scales, see the grass grow,
And fly with better than Icarian wings
From Rome to Thule."

    Pro.   Had he any guess
Of how the world was made ?

     Dru.   "Too deep for thought,"
He said, "much more for language."   Yet he mused
And question'd thus, "The nature of the Whole
Moved, and began the order'd Universe ;
And everything must be continuous
From that prime impulse.   Shall we deem this force,
Ev'n in the highest things whereto it tendeth,
Void of a rational principle ?—or all
From one divine inscrutable First Cause,
Whence too our rational being must derive
Its powers ?   The order that subsists in thee
Is under rule of reason.   Can this rule
Be absent in the Universe ?   Not so.
One Living Mind rules all."

    Pro.   Remember'd well !
I see this as I never saw before.
His words are precious gems.   Doth Commodus
Set forth at once to Rome ?   What think'st thou of
     him ?
The slaves are out of hearing.

    Dru.   Grant me this,
Dear friend, no word of politics to-night !

    Pro. So be it.   Tell me more then of our Prince
Who now is with the Gods.

     Dru.   Oft in his tent

Or by a watchfire on the battle-field,
I saw him take a little parchment-scroll
Out of his bosom ; and on a certain night
He let me look therein, close-writ in Greek ;
Saying, " I put these thoughts upon my tablets
As they came to me, wrote them fairly out,
And turn to them again from time to time ;
Since what is written, even by oneself,
Becomes a force, takes place in the world of things,
And may be found again and scann'd again ;
Thus wise mood and clear insight come in aid
Of weak dark moments, and hold judgment firm.
The most," he said, " were written long ago ;
I read in them my brighter healthier self ;
Now, things grow wearisome, and seldom seem
Worth the style's labour—yet are they no worse,
No better than of old." With leave, I conn'd
The sentences, and copied many down
In our own tongue from memory. Words are seeds.
Here is my scroll, if thou art not yet tired.
But much he spoke was to the same effect.
    Pro. Nay, read, Drusillus.
    Dru.   Thus Aurelius :
" Whate'er it be, this Universe,—myself
Am part thereof, related intimately
To other parts like me, my fellow-men.
Let me be thankful and content, and seek
The common good ; for happy he alone
Who, wise in contemplation, just in action,
Resigns himself to universal nature,
Expecting, fearing, and disliking nothing,
And puts his ruling faculty to use.
Ask this—how doth the ruling faculty
Employ itself ? All else is but as smoke."—
" What is this hubbub that goes on around ?
Vain pomp and stage-play, weapon-brandishings,
Sheep following sheep (poor men !), herds driv'n along,

Dogs rushing to a bone, fish to a crumb,
Labours of ants, hurry of fright'n'd mice,
The posturing of puppets pull'd by strings!
View it all quietly, good-naturedly,
And not with scorn; but clearly understand
A man is worth so much as that is worth
He busies himself in.   Yet, all are brethren:
Turn not away from any man or thing."—
"Wrong-doers must be, therefore marvel not
To meet one; he's in error; on thy part
Seek to amend him kindly: if thou'rt anger'd
Give thyself blame, not him.   Be not perturb'd.
If a man hate thee, that is his affair,
Thine, that he have no cause.   Upon thyself
Depends thy happiness; thy will is free;
Obey the voice of God."—Mark this, my friend:
"If God had plann'd it all—enough: art thou
Wiser than God?   But certain men surmise
Chance ruleth all, or Fate: be thou at least
Not rulèd so, and having cared for this,
Be tranquil."   Note that, Probus—"Thou at least
Be not so rulèd."   Often would he say,
"What is the dearest, most essential thing,
Whereof can no man rob us?   Our Free-Will!"
   Pro. A grand word!   But, how choose therewith?
   Dru.   He held,
That, as our lungs inhale the atmosphere,
A subtler spiritual force pervades the world,
Which he who wills may draw into his mind.
   Pro. Strange!—yet my soul breathes freer at his
     words.
Read on.
   Dru. In this the perfect Stoic speaks:
"Rule thy opinion, and thou rulest all
Comes from without; esteem that as it is,
Nothing—the Ruling Faculty untouch'd."
   Pro. I am too weak for that!

Dru.   Again he writes :
" Value not life at any costly rate,
Reflect : the Past a dream, the Future nothing,
The Present is the only thing thou hast,
Therefore the only thing which thou can'st lose,
And what is that ?—a point."
       Pro.   The sophist here
Methinks, Drusillus—subtlety for wisdom !
The Past is *in* the Present, and the point
Is moving, therefore measureless.
       Dru.   Well said !
No man is always right.
       Pro.   And then, " Opinion ? "
Suppose at some bad inn I drink sour wine,
How shall opinion make me taste and feel
Falernian ? Or should angry Neptune toss
My wretched body, hath opinion power
To comfort me ?
       Dru.   Some men are tougher made
No doubt, than others ; for the perfect Stoic
Too nice a palate is unapt, too weak
A stomach ; yet the main point lies not here.
Make by our Ruling Faculty the least
And not the most of adverse accident,
The best and not the worst of all our gifts,
We're followers, though with feeble step it be,
Of Zeno, Epictetus, and Aurelius.
Live but to gratify our lower selves :
And study these, we're on the hateful road
With Nero and his parasites.
       Pro.   A gloss
On Stoicism !—a good one I allow.
I fear I'm of the sons of Epicurus—
The later sons, degenerate from his doctrine !
       Dru. Nay, thou malign'st thyself—in vain to me.
No two men are alike, nor no two Stoics.
But here are maxims fit for every man :

"Act as thy nature leads, observing justice.
Rate everything according to its value.
Bear what the common nature brings to thee."
"Study not what thy neighbour says, does, thinks,
But live thine own life rightly. Talk no more
Of how a man should live, but so live thou."—
"The Soul's a sphere, and keeps her proper shape
If not stretch'd forth to outward things too far,
Nor, else, contracted inward, shrunk together.
"Seek imperturbably to live a life
Of wisdom, justice, temperance, fortitude;
Be ever friendly, mild, benevolent;
And follow thy eudæmon—God within thee."

  Pro. Gold words! The sweetest of the Stoics, he.
Unless it were his Father.
  Dru.   Nay, for him
Good life sufficed, without philosophy.
  Pro. Little have I of either! But note this;
Marcus's nature, that was rational,
Mild, kind and sociable; the voice within
Counsell'd him good not evil things. We all
Are not so made. Some men are idly given,
Care but for feasts and flowers and fluteplayers;
Why should they baulk their fancies? Others
  thirst
For glory, praise, and power; and why not seek
  them,
Such being their nature? How fit every man
To Marcus?
  Dru.   Ay, or any other pattern?
I said, no two alike, each his own life;
And yet must none live solely for himself.
The idle and the grasping miss true life
Through error; help them; for, as Plato wrote,
Willingly is no soul deprived of truth;
Count all amendable.
  Pro.   Nay, some I know

In whom a cacodæmon surely whispers!
How deal with these?
 Dru.   Shun, guard against, repress;
At utmost need, expel them solemnly,
As curs'd by fate or their perverted wills,
And give them over to the larger Power.
Aurelius could be stern—but ever sadly.
Yet, tho' in his self-judgment strict, and all
That touch'd the State, to other men at times
(Perhaps because he did not rate them high)
And women, he was far too mild, too easy;
His only fault. Witness his former colleague.
Witness his—— But enough. His life was pure,
His death was tranquil. May our souls tread firm
To follow his!
 Pro. Alas, I would the Gods, .
Spoke out with clearer voice to us poor men
On life and death! How should our souls be firm
When oracles are doubtful?—Will new Cæsar
Follow the fierce Bellona's flashing helm?
Dru. Not if he hold his father's counsel dear.
"Jove grant my son," Aurelius used to say,
"Have little need and no desire of war.
War I detest. Yet I have lived in war,
To keep Augustus Cæsar's legacy,
Our empire's bounds, unbroken—on the west
The Atlantic Ocean, on the north the Rhine
And Danube, with Euphrates to the east,
Africa's burning deserts to the south;
The savage isle of Britain join'd to these
By later outpulse of imperial force,
And Hadrian's Dacia afterwards. War—war—"
Would he exclaim, "I hate war—could not shun
  it!
O happy Antoninus, fitly named
The Pious, three-and-twenty peaceful years
The lifting of thy sceptre sway'd the world,

No further journeying than Lanuvium !"
  Two months ago, as many times before,
He spake in this wise ; and, on that same evening,
Came I for orders to the Emperor.
And found him pacing lonely on the bank
Of the broad Danube in a wintry dusk.
My business done, he lifted up his eyes,
And seeing great stars rising in the east,
"Think of the courses of the heavens," he said,
"The boundless gulf of past and future time,
And what our little lives are.   This whole Earth
We move upon is but a point."   He stept
Silent some way, then stopping short exclaimed—
"Who can believe that good and noble souls,
The highest things we wot of, when they leave us
Perish and are extinguished, or that God
Will not preserve them, if the general scheme
Allow thereof?   This body is not me ;
'Tis but the vessel and the instrument
Of an imperishable essence ; yea,
Myself and God are under one same law."
He ceased, then added in a lower voice—
"Shall man dispute with God?   O reverence Him
Confide in Him who governs everything !
The perfect living Being, good and just
And beautiful, who generates, who holds
Together all things, who contains them all,
Continually dissolved and reproduced,
Himself not changed ; from whom the soul of man
Is drawn, an efflux of the Deity."
When next I saw Marcus Aurelius,
He lay in fever.
    Pro.   Did it long endure?
    Dru. I'll tell thee, Probus.   On the fifteenth day
I watch'd him, kneeling by the couch.   His mind
Had wander'd, but he now lay motionless,
As in a trance, from noon till the fifth hour.

All unexpectedly, he looked upon me.
Forth came his hand.   I kiss'd it.   My heart leapt
With a pang of fleeting joy.   He merely said—
"Farewell, Drusillus.   Bear the news to Rome."
Then his eyes closed again ; and no more words.
        Pro. Young Commodus, I think——
        Dru.   I think, my friend,
He had a virtuous and most noble Father.
        Pro. Truly.   And I for my part recollect
Caligula's father was Germanicus,
Domitian's Titus.   But—Hail, Commodus !
Cæsar and Emperor, seventeenth in count
From shrewd Augustus—some amongst them great
And many vile.   Fortune hath strangely throned
Pernicious human monsters, gorging blood
Until it choked them.
        Dru.   Yea, but Rome endures ;
Jove's oak, whereon some carrion vultures perch'd ;
Empire that was, and is, and will be great ;
Never before so powerful, and so happy
As under Trajan, Hadrian, Antonine,
And our beloved Aurelius.
        Pro.   And yet,
All things, Drusillus, have their term.   Jove's oak,
Rock-rooted, wide-arm'd, after many years
Grows hollow, one day crumbles.   Shall men see
Great Rome a ruin ?
        Dru.   Choose more lucky words,
Dear Probus !—or indeed wilt thou forebode
This Christian superstition, the crush'd worm,
Lord of our seven hills, with superber shrine
Than Jove's own temple now ? or dost thou fear
The Britons may outrival us in arms,
Wealth, power, and policy, and one day build
A greater city than on Tiber's banks
By some cold fenny river of the north ?
        Pro. Nay, I love Rome.   Live Rome !

Dru.   She'll outlast *us*,
Be who will Cæsar.   May the Gods protect her!
Thanks and farewell, my friend!
     Pro.   The slaves await you.
Health and sound sleep, Drusillus!   Fare thee well!

———————

A NURSERY RHYME FOR THE ELDERS.

THE Masters of the World when we are gone
 Play round our knees, look up to us with awe,
  From our lips take their earliest deepest law;
In jest we mould the clay that turns to stone,
Give little care what sort of seed is sown,
  What weeds therewith, or venoms. If we saw
The Future, with our part distinctly shown,
  Vulture Remorse might tear us, beak and claw.

Dolt! Coward! Rogue! must Ages yet to be
 Inherit, with Life's necessary griefs,
What thou thyself perceivest base in thee?—
  Factitious crimes and duties, sham beliefs,
  Pride like a murderer's, pleasure like a thief's
Man's very best besteep'd in falsity!

GRAVES AND URNS

IN SHADOW.

WHO with set eyelids venturing into years
    That are not come, like years of long ago,
Can warm those shadows? Dusk, with steps as slow
As mine, crept through the Graveyard, dropping tears
Like one that mourn'd. I mused and mused: me-
    thought
Some months, some years were gone, and evening
    brought
To linger by these graves a pensive Boy.
Amid the twilight stillness deep and lone
He stoops to read an old half-buried stone,
And weeds the mosses that almost destroy
The letters of the name, which is—my own.
The wind about the old gray tower makes moan.
He rises from the grave with sadden'd brow,
Leaving it to the night, and sighs, as I do now.

HIS TOWN.

HIS Town is one of memory's haunts,—
　　Shut in by fields of corn and flax,
Like housings gay on elephants
　　Heaved on the huge hill-backs.

How pleasantly that image came!
　　As down the zigzag road I press'd,
Blithe, but unable yet to claim
　　His roof from all the rest.

And I should see my Friend at home,
　　Be in the little town at last
Those welcome letters dated from,
　　Gladdening the two years past.

I recollect the summer-light,
　　The bridge with poplars at its end,
The slow brook turning left and right,
　　The greeting of my Friend.

I found him; he was mine,—his books,
　　His home, his day, his favourite walk,
The joy of swift-conceiving looks,
　　The glow of living talk.

July, no doubt, comes brightly still
　　On blue-eyed flax and yellowing wheat;
But sorrow shadows vale and hill
　　Since one heart ceased to beat.

Is not the climate colder there,
    Since that Youth died?—it must be so;
A dumb regret is in the air;
    The brook repines to flow.

Wing'd thither, fancy only sees
    An old church on its rising ground,
And underneath two sycamore trees
    A little grassy mound.

THE CRUCIBLE.

I

IS he shrunk to Name and Date,
    Painted on a coffin plate?

II.

With golden talismans bedeck'd,
Deep this single man was sheathed
In atmosphere of soft respect,
Which everyone around him breathed.
Well he was served, well attended,
Well becourted, well befriended ;
Many labours stopt or sped
By the turning of his head ;
Many lives toil'd like bees
To make the honey of his ease.

III.

And leave you *him* all alone
Beneath a stone,
Now when comes the twilight cold
Down the bare wold,
And winds are crying to the darken'd foam ;
When thoughts of glowing rooms and faces
And the dear domestic graces
Draw all men home?
On this stone the ragged rooks will meet,
The gusty rain-storm rave and beat,

The little grass-mouse will scamper over it
To and from her nest in the bield,
The wide-falling winter snow will cover it,
With other stones of the field.
Black Rook, white Snow, how can they know
This stone has a costly vault below?
Brown Mouse, wild Rain, 'tis too, too plain,
Won't spare this grave from the common disdain.

IV.

Oh, you say it is not he
You are laying by the sea;
Leaving in the graveyard lonely;
'Tis not he—his body only.
Darkness is its dwelling fit,
And a stone to cover it.
He Himself, His Soul, you say,
God has call'd him far away.

V.

Would that men would well discern
What a lesson they might learn
From this natural separation,
Chemist Death's elimination
Of the drossy and the fleeting,
Past all further trick or cheating;
And in the actual be so wise
As to justly analyse
The elements of life, while blended,
Which they rank, when all is ended,
Thus concluded, proved, and past,
In a truer rate at last.
Long his Life : and in the whole
How much worship earn'd his Soul?

THE COLD WEDDING.

BUT few days gone
        Her hand was won
By suitor finely skill'd to woo;
    And now come we
        In pomp to see
The Church's ceremonials due.

    The Bride in white
        Is clad aright,
Within her carriage closely hid;
    No blush to veil—
        For too, too pale
The cheek beneath each downcast lid.

    White favours rest
        On every breast;
And yet methinks we seem not gay.
    The church is cold,
        The priest is old,—
But who will give the bride away?

    Now delver, stand,
        With spade in hand,
All mutely to discharge thy trust:
    Priest's words sound forth;
        They're—" Earth to earth,
" Ashes to ashes, dust to dust."

The groom is Death;
He has no breath;
(The wedding peals, how slow they swing!)
With icy grip
He soon will clip
Her finger with a wormy ring.

A match most fair,
This silent pair,
Now to each other given for ever,
Were lovers long,
Were plighted strong
In oaths and bonds that could not sever.

Ere she was born
That vow was sworn;
And we must lose into the ground
Her face we knew:
As thither you
And I, and all, are swiftly bound.

This Law of Laws
That still withdraws
Each mortal from all mortal ken—
If 'twere not here;
Or we saw clear
Instead of dim as now; what then?
This were not Earth, and we not Men.

PHANTAST.

"The monument woos me."
Second Maiden's Tragedy.

EVERYTHING that seeks to do thee harm
   Hearkens to the song that I am singing.
Sly and winding worm is in his hole,
Ruddy shrewmice listen in their burrow;
Wasps are nested by thee, but the charm
Keeps that yellow robber-band from stinging;
In thy bed of clay the howking mole
Bores no tunnel thorough.
     Now that day from heaven is gone,
     Thou art smoothly dreaming on,—
     Not to waken with the dawn.

Only now the moaning of the breeze
Answers to the song that I am singing.
In the moonlit dyke the crouching hare
Raises up her watchful ears to listen;
From the blackness of the ghostly trees
Swift and silent bats like Dreams are winging,
Round the grassy hummocks here and there
Elfin tapers glisten.
     Whilst the wind's sad tale is told,
     Thou art lapt up from the cold
     In a blanket made of mould.

Many nights and many days have heard
Songs of mine like this that I am singing;
By the sun, or by this paler round;
In the dark, when shrouded stars are weeping;
When the old tower shakes his ivy-beard,
When the skiey thunder-bells are ringing;
Hurtful things that live below the ground
From thy pillow keeping.
    And when I have leave to die,
    Then an Angel from the sky
    Comes to watch us where we lie.

IN HIGHGATE CEMETERY.

FAR-SPREAD below doth LONDON wear
    Its cloud by day, its fire by night;
But scarce with heavenly presence there,
    Enshrined in smoke or pallid light.

Incessant troops from that vast throng
    Withdraw to silent colonies;
Where houses, lo, are fair and strong,
    Though ruins all that dwell in these.

Yet here, too, under boundless sky,
    Do children sport, and wild birds sing;
Calm foliage waxes green and high,
    And grave-side roses smell of Spring.

THE FUNERAL

SAY not we "bury him;" nor talk
  Of "sleeping in the tomb."
With foolish words the soul we baulk,
  And shut it round with gloom.

The mystic form whereby we knew
  Our parent once, or friend,
Let this, indeed, have reverence due
  For life's sake, tho' at end.

But this no more is man at all,
  Mere water now and clay,
Fit to be purged by fire, or fall
  Apart in slow decay.

Life—Death—are hieroglyphics writ,
  By one mysterious hand,
Their meaning passes all our wit,
  We may not understand.

Forget men's timid vain pretence,
  Forget their babbling speech;
Trust to thy Spirit's highest sense
  The truest faith to reach.

URN BURIAL.

EARTH is too full of graves,
  So is Man's Mind :
Must we be always slaves,
  Self-shackled, blind ?

Like fierce Mezentius, tie
  Living to Dead ?
No !—let flame purify
  The foul instead,—

Purge quickly soil and air,
  Body and soul,
Of base obstruction there,
  In man's control,—

Give thus, for horror and pest,
  Some ashes, white
As snow or sea-wave's crest
  Or still moonlight,
Or thoughts of the loved and blest
  Withdrawn from sight.

FORWARD.

I.

EVER streams the living gale
    To some forward goal,
Forward, forward bends our sail,
    Forward strains our soul.

II.

Grandly of the ways of men,
Guesses childhood.   But since then
Master Time has made me free,
Step by step in swift advance,
Of manhood's full freemasonry ;
And its mysteries prove to be
Blanker far than ignorance.

III.

Men have a narrow range of sight,
A little peristyle of light,
A world of thought confused and crude,
Where chaos still is unsubdued.
Soothed in daily pain and sorrow,
With nursery promise for to-morrow,
They dream of corners unexplored
Where the wealth of life is stored,
Something to be shown at last,
Something to be known at last,
Beyond these poor toys of the Present ;
Moon of hope, for ever crescent,
Seems to grow, is never grown.

IV.

Yet for the weakest one of these,
All the Arabian mysteries
Within the world's most credulous scope,
Afford not space enough for Hope
To build the Future's temple in :
At last they end where those begin,
Who searching with a mountain-view
The old earth-world all round and round,
And nowhere finding open ground,
At once send Hope on strong wings forth
Into a world almost as new as birth,—
Hope saith, *almost* as new.

V.

And so at last, not much afraid,
Forward, file on file, we march
Into the gloom which takes our breath ;
Nay when the Sun with glance divine
Upon that tearful cloud may shine,
Behold a new triumphal arch—
Yea, see the very Door of Death
   Out of a Rainbow made !

WOULD I KNEW!

PLAYS a child in a garden fair
　　Where the demigods are walking;
Playing unsuspected there
As a bird within the air,
　　Listens to their wondrous talking:
"Would I knew—would I knew
What it is they say and do!"

Stands a youth at city-gate,
　　Sees the knights go forth together,
Parleying superb, elate,
Pair by pair in princely state,
　　Lance and shield and haughty feather:
"Would I knew—would I knew
What it is they say and do!"

Bends a man with trembling knees
　　By a gulf of cloudy border;
Deaf, he hears no voice from these
Wingèd shades he dimly sees
　　Passing by in solemn order:
"Would I knew—O would I knew
What it is they say and do!"

DEATH DEPOSED.

I.

DEATH stately came to a young man, and said
              " If thou wert dead,
What matter?"   The young man replied,
              " See my young bride,
Whose life were all one blackness if I died.
My land requires me ; and the world's self, too,
Methinks, would miss some things that I can do."

II.

Then Death in scorn this only said,
              " Be dead,"
And so he was.   And soon another's hand
              Made rich his land.
The sun, too, of three summers had the might
To bleach the widow's hue, light and more light,
              Again to bridal white.
And nothing seem'd to miss beneath that sun
              His work undone.

III.

But Death soon met another man, whose eye
              Was Nature's spy ;
Who said, " Forbear thy too triumphant scorn.
              The weakest born
Of all the sons of men, is by his birth
Heir of the Might Eternal ; and this Earth
Is subject to him in his place.
              Thou leav'st no trace.

IV.

" Thou,—the mock Tyrant that men fear and hate,
            Grim fleshless Fate,
Cold, dark, and wormy thing of loss and tears?
            Not in the sepulchres
Thou dwellest, but in my own crimson'd heart ;
Where while it beats we call thee Life.   Depart !
A name, a shadow, into any gulf,
Out of this world, which is not thine,
            But mine :
        Or stay !—because thou art
            Only Myself."

NO funeral gloom, my dears, when I am gone,
   Corpse-gazings, tears, black raiment, graveyard
      grimness ;
Think of me as withdrawn into the dimness,
Yours still, you mine ; remember all the best
Of our past moments, and forget the rest ;
   And so, to where I wait, come gently on.

A POET'S EPITAPH.

BODY to purifying flame,
  Soul to the Great Deep whence it came,
Leaving a song on earth below,
An urn of ashes white as snow.

WHAT is your Heaven? describe it in a breath.
  Pure health, fit work, beyond the gate of death.

THE FIRST ENGLISH POET

Discern this Soul, his time and his abode:
In such a mould his reverent musings flow'd.

6—2

THE FIRST ENGLISH POET.

DWELT a certain poor man in his day,
   Near at hand to Hilda's holy house,
Learning's lighthouse, blessed beacon, built
High o'er sea and river, on the head,
Streaneshalch in Anglo-Saxon speech,
Whitby, after, by the Norsemen named.
Cædmon was he call'd ; he came and went,
Doing humble duties for the monks,
Helping with the horses at behest ;
Modest, meek, unmemorable man,
Moving slowly into middle age,
Toiling on,—twelve hundred years ago.

   Still and silent, Cædmon sometimes sat
With the serfs at lower end of hall ;
There he marvell'd much to hear the monks
Singing sweetly hymns unto their harp,
Handing it from each to each in turn,
Till his heart-strings trembled.   Otherwhile,
When the serfs were merry with themselves,
Sung their folk-songs upon festal nights,
Handing round the harp to each in turn,
Cædmon, though he loved not lighter songs,
Long'd to sing,—but he could never sing.

   Sad and silent would he creep away,
Wander forth alone, he wist not why,
Watch the sky and water, stars or clouds
Climbing from the sea ; and in his soul
Shadows mounted up and mystic lights,

Echoes vague and vast return'd the voice
Of the rushing river, roaring waves,
Twilight's windy whisper from the fells,
Howl of brindled wolf, and cry of bird ;
Every sight and sound of solitude
Ever mingling in a master thought,
Glorious, terrible, of the Mighty One
Who made all things.   As the Book declared.
"*In the Beginning He made Heaven and Earth.*"

Thus lived Cædmon, quiet year by year;
Listen'd, learn'd a little, as he could ;
Work'd, and mused, and pray'd, and held his peace.

Toward the end of harvest time, the hinds
Held a feast, and sung their festal songs,
Handing round the harp from each to each.
But before it came where Cædmon sat,
Sadly, silently, he stole away,
Wander'd to the stable-yard and wept,
Weeping laid him low among the straw,
Fell asleep at last.   And in his sleep
Came a Stranger, calling him by name :
" Cædmon, sing to me !"   " I cannot sing.
Wherefore—wo is me !—I left the house."
"Sing, I bid thee !"   "What then shall I sing ?"
"Sing the Making of the World."   Whereon
Cædmon sung : and when he woke from sleep
Still the verses stay'd with him, and more
Sprang like fountain-water from a rock
Fed from never-failing secret springs.

Praising Heaven most high, but nothing proud,
Cædmon sought the Steward and told his tale,
Who to Holy Hilda led him in,
Pious Princess Hilda, pure of heart,
Ruling Mother, royal Edwin's niece.

Cædmon at her bidding boldly sang
Of the Making of the World, in words
Wondrous; whereupon they wotted well
'Twas an Angel taught him, and his gift
Came direct from God : and glad were they.

Thenceforth Holy Hilda greeted him
Brother of the brotherhood.   He grew
Famedest monk of all the monastery ;
Singing many high and holy songs
Folk were fain to hear, and loved him for :
Till his death-day came, that comes to all.

Cædmon bode that evening in his bed,
He at peace with men and men with him ;
Wrapt in comfort of the Eucharist ;
Weak and silent.   "Soon our Brethren sing
Evensong?" he whisper'd.   " Brother, yea."
" Let us wait for that," he said ; and soon
Sweetly sounded up the solemn chant.
Cædmon smiled and listen'd ; when it lull'd,
Sidelong turn'd to sleep his old white head,
Shut his eyes, and gave his soul to God,
Maker of the World.

                        Twelve hundred years
Since are past and gone, nor he forgot,
Earliest Poet of the English Race.
Rude and simple were his days and thoughts.
Wisely speaketh no man, howso learn'd,
Of the making of this wondrous World,
Save a Poet, with a reverent soul.

PRESENT-FUTURE.

"GIVE back my youth !" the poets cry,
   "Give back my youth !"—so say not I.
Youth play'd its part with us ; if we
Are losers, should we gainers be
By recommencing, with the same
Conditions, all the finish'd game ?
If we see better now, we are
Already winners just so far,—
And merely ask to keep our winning,
Wipe out loss, for new beginning !
This may come, in Heaven's good way,
How, no mortal man shall say ;
But not by fresh-recover'd taste
For sugarplums or valentines,
Or conjuring back the brightest day
Which gave its gift and therefore shines.
Win or lose, possess or miss,
There cannot be a weaker waste
Of memory's privilege than this—
To dwell among cast-off designs,
Stages, larvæ of yourself,
And leave the true thing on the shelf,
The Present-Future, wherewith blend
Hours that hasten to their end.

I.

ART thou Lórd of the World?   Was it all made
for thee,
  Child of Time, Child of Clay?
Thinkest thou, skies will ever bend o'er thee,
  Bland and friendly as those of to-day?
      Every joy its savour keep,
      Night o'erflow with happy sleep,
      Pain and sorrow shun thy roof,
      Sad Old Age keep well aloof,
      Life go smoothly on its way,
      Brain control, and hand obey,
      To-morrow be like yesterday?

II.

      Things only wait, they only wait,
      They lie in ambush for thy fate.
      Days go, and nights go,
      Years run away, and lo!
      Now the end is coming fast
      The proud foolish dream past;
      See the brand, so brightly kindled,
      To a fading ember dwindled,
      All thy pleasures, all thy riches,
      Vanish like a dance of witches!

III.

Is this indeed the revolt thou wert fearing,
  Child of the Infinite, Child of Hope?
Or is it the lower world disappearing
  Whilst thou art lifted to higher scope?
      Thou, as needs, art drawn away.
      Think,—truly,—would'st thou stay?
      Nothing has been given thee yet
      So good, but better thou may'st get.

EVERYDAY.

LET us not teach and preach so much,
  But cherish, rather than profess;
Be careful how the thoughts we touch
  Of God, and Love, and Holiness.

A charm, most spiritual, faint,
  And delicate, forsakes our breast,
Bird-like, when it perceives the taint
  Of prying breath upon its nest.

Using, enjoying, let us live;
  Set here to grow, what should we do
But take what soil and climate give?
  For thence must come our sap and hue:

Blooming as sweetly as we may,
  Nor beckon comers, nor debar;
Let them take balm or gall away,
  According as their natures are:

Look straight at all things from the soul,
  But boast not much to understand;
Make each new action sound and whole,
  Then leave it in its place unscann'd:

Be true, devoid of aim or care;
  Nor posture, nor antagonise:
Know well that clouds of this our air
  But seem to wrap the mighty skies:

Search starry mysteries overhead,
  Where wonders gleam; yet bear in mind
That Earth's our planet, firm to tread,
  Nor in the star-dance left behind:

For nothing is withheld, be sure,
    Our being needed to have shown ;
The far was meant to be obscure,
    The near was placed so to be known.

Cast we no astrologic scheme
    To map the course we must pursue ;
But use the lights whene'er they beam,
    And every trusty landmark too.

The Future let us not permit
    To choke us in its shadow's clasp ;
It cannot touch us, nor we it ;
    The present moment's in our grasp.

Soul sever'd from the Truth is Sin ;
    The dark and dizzy gulf is Doubt ;
Truth never moves,—unmoved therein,
    Our road is straight and firm throughout.

This Road for ever doth abide.
    The universe, if fate so call,
May sink away on either side ;
    But This and God at once shall fall

Ashby Manor.

A PLAY.

To

MY WIFE.

ACT I.—*June 14, 1645.*

SCENE 1.—Stable yard of Ashby Manor House, Northamptonshire.
(Sunlight.)

SCENE 2.—Room in the Manor House.
(Daylight.)

ACT II.—*A day in September, same year.*

SCENE 1.—Anteroom in the Manor House, opening on a Terrace, with harvest view.
(Warm evening light.)

SCENE 2.—Fine old Room or Gallery in the same, with pictures, armour, &c.
(Dusk, and afterwards candles.)

PERSONS.

BASIL RADCLYFFE (about 50), Colonel of Horse for Parliament under General Ireton.

CHARLTON RADCLYFFE, his nephew (about 28, handsome, but gloomy and ill-tempered), Captain in the same Regiment.

GEORGE FORTESCUE, afterwards LORD LYNDORE (about 24), Royalist Cavalry Officer, under Prince Rupert.

TOM TRIVET, his servant, an honest Devonshire lad, a trooper in the same Regiment.

CORPORAL GHOME (a sleek rascal), in Captain Radclyffe's troop.

SIR THOMAS CHENERY (dignified elderly man), Commissioner of the Parliament.

MR. JOHN CHAD, lawyer, his Secretary (keen lawyer, with rigid features).

CORNET JEBB, Parliamentarian (self-conceited).

JERRY, a youth.   Old CROOKES, an aged servitor.

MISTRESS RADCLYFFE (a beautiful woman of 40 or 42), wife of the Colonel.

NAOMI RADCLYFFE (about 20), their only child.

PRUDENCE, a waiting-woman.

JERUSHA, a dairymaid.

Other servants.   Troopers.

7

ASHBY MANOR.

*Before the curtain rises, military music or overture, with drums and
trumpet : a march and battle-piece (including "Prince Rupert's
March"), dying off at last, and ending with two trumpet-calls ;
the second more distant, replying to the other. N.B.—All the
Music with this Play ought to be English, of the 16th and 17th
centuries.]*

THE PROLOGUE.

(Spoken before the Curtain.)

A TREMBLING Author—use him kindly, pray !—
  Presents to you to-night his first essay.
'Tis all his own—words, characters, and plot ;
But all is nothing, if it please you not.
Then *try* to like it ; half the battle's there !
And you, fair Ladies, O be more than fair
In this, be generous to him ; recognize
His good intentions with indulgent eyes ;
And though he cannot picture womanhood
A thousandth part as richly as he would
If love and reverence might suffice,—with aid
Of sympathy, he'll show you, less afraid,
An English Daughter and an English Wife,
Toss'd on the angry waves of civil strife,
Yet never losing heart, when England fought
Against herself, and for herself, distraught
Yet full of reason, wisely mad, and sent
For either party, King and Parliament,
Most precious lives into the bloody field,
Most honest men on both sides. Can you yield
Your thought on fancy's wings to float away
To Charles's time, a byegone summer day
At Naseby ?—Now the roar of fight is done ;
The curtain rises ; and our scene's begun.

[Exit.

ACT I.—SCENE I.

Afternoon of June 14, 1645. Stable yard of Ashby Manor-house, Northamptonshire; half-timbered Elizabethan out-buildings; roofs and chimneys of the Manor-house rising beyond. Large gate, and practicable Wicket, R. Stable with practicable door, L.

Enter cautiously, opening the wicket, a young Cavalier (with helmet, cuirass and gorget, sword, riding boots, &c.) and his Servant, a trooper (without sword). They look soiled and tired. Cavalier's right arm tied up with a red sash, as wounded.

George Fortescue. All seems quiet here.

Tom Trivet. Good luck 'twas unbolted, zir.

G. F. Make it fast. A friendly house, think you?

[TOM *bolts wicket.*

Tom. That's to prove, zir. An they be king's volk, better for we. If not, we must hide zomewheres and slink out i' th' dimmet. Wish we could borrow a dark ne'at vrom Christmas next!

[*Looks round about.*

G. F. How far are we from Naseby village?

Tom. Zome dree mile, zir, a' 'ood zay.

G. F. Hiding and slinking are not much to my taste, Tom.

Tom. They bean't Devonsheer tricks, your honour! but luck's again us, and the Roundheads after us.

G. F. Confound them!

Tom. 'Oss, voot and dragoons! Zimmeth these New-Noddle men can vight, zir?—London 'prentices and jitch-like, we was told.

G. F. Ha, they can fight! How Cromwell's horsemen thundered in! But, Tom,—this letter for his Highness the Prince of Wales, which his Majesty's own hand gave into mine: it must be delivered at all risks.

Tom. Could we a' kept out o' thik last unlucky scrimmage, we should a' bin well on our wa-y to Exeter

Wicket.   From the House.   ACT I. SC. I.   From the Dairy.   Shed.   Stable.

by now. O zweet Devonsheer! (*G. F. touches his
wounded arm*). Your honour's arm paineth?

G. F. Not very much. Here, Tom, shift my sword-
belt to t'other side.

Tom. (*Doing it.*) Would your honour vight left-
handed?

G. F. Sooner than be taken by a clown with a hayfork.

Tom. Fegs, a'd 's lieve not veace hayfork at the
present minnit! My weepon's gone: a'll tek' thea-
samy in case o' need. (*Picks up an axe for chopping
wood.*) Zomebody's a comin'.—In, zir, vor God's sake!
[*They hide behind an outhouse*, L.

Enter JERUSHA (*2nd entrance* L) *as from milking, with
two pails. She sets them down and shakes her
head.*

J. The very cows, poor things, are frighted out o'
their wits, and no wonder. It bean't 'alf a proper milking, and th' noise o' them great guns is enow to turn
sower what there is o't. It do turn my blood into
buttermilk!

Enter PRUDENCE *as from house* (centre).

J. O Prue!

P. O Jerusha!

J. Ah, you may well say so!

P. What times we live in!

J. I wish we'd been a-born in other times!

P. Our fathers and mothers lived and died in their
beds; not like this wicked Civil War!

J. I see no civility in't. Master away fighting;
John and Timothy and Jenkyn away fighting, and
our five best horses, and ne'er a man left but Gaffer
Crookes, and Jerry, and our young lady's pet mare.

P. And Mistress in her room there (*points towards house*) praying, praying, as well as she can for them roaring cannon bullets all the marning. Be they done at last, think you?

J. I've heerd none these two hours.

P. Thank goodness for that!—And the dear Young Mistress, talking cheerful to everybody, wi' her eyes full of tears. If our folk on'y gets safe back, all's well.

J. May the Lord guard them!

P. Maybe they're all murdered!

J. O dear!

P. Lying stiff and bloody in the grass—

J. Don't talk so!

P. Or crying out for someone to gi'e 'em a drink o' water.   [*Shots heard.*

Both. Oh! oh!   [*They weep. Enter* JERRY, *a youth, breathless.*

Jerry. News! news!

P. What is it, Jerry? Where hast been? Speak!

Jer. News, great news! A've bin at th' great foight.

J. You!

Jer. Ay, *me*, and a've run all th' way back.

P. That's true, I warrant.

Jer. Not till the King and his foine gentry ran away first. We've a-bait 'em, girls, we've a-bait em! Victory! The Ironsides for ever!

J. How was it?

P. Is master safe?

J. And Jenkyn?

P. And Timothy?

J. And all?

P Didst see them?

J. Come they straight back?

P. Is anybody killed?

J. Or wounded?

        [*They put these questions quickly;* JERRY *turns from one to the other.*

P. Spaik out, man!

J. Quick!

Jer. There's another question you've not asked me.

J. What's that?

Jer. If I be hungry and thirsty. Get me a quart of ale, and then—

P. Run, Jerusha! (*She goes.*) And some cold roast pork, too. But say, Jerry, is anyone hurt?

[JERUSHA *returns with ale.*

J. O, is anyone hurt?

Jer. Many a one. (*Drinks.*) But nōne of our house. Leastwise, I hopes not.

P. You hopes not!—Did you see master?

Jer. No.

J. Or Jenkyn, or Timothy?

Jer. Ay.

J. Lord be praised! When come they back?

Jer. Hm—hm—

P. Answer, stupid!

Jer. Not a word more, stupid as I am, till I sees my mistress. But this much a'll tell ye—

Both. Yes!

Jer. I've awful things to tell——

Both. Ah!

Jer. But not to you. (*Female voice heard calling from house.*) I'm too long here! (*Runs off* (C), *they follow, crying out, " Jerry! Jerry!"*)

Re-enter (L) *Cavalier and* TOM.

Tom. A dale o' chatter, but I coodn' hear what 'twas 'bout. How vare you, zir?

G. F. Well enough—considering.

Tom. Zems to me, your honour, we be all ruinated, vrom King down.

G. F. Nay, Tom, we'll turn tables on these Roundheads yet.

Tom. We've a-zung to thik tune long while!—and we 'ave a be-at 'em too, but tha' doozen' zem to mind it—not bein' men of honour, like.

G. F. When our side's beaten, we feel it.

Tom. (*Rubbing his shoulder.*) Zartinly we does! We be on raight zide, measter George, bean't us?

G. F. I hope so, Tom. Hush, sirrah! draw in hither.   [*They approach a door, near front.* L,

TOM *peeps through hole in door.*

Tom. A stable, and a hoss in't. Well, a hoss han't no politics—there! (*Opens door; then stands in door-way.*) Soho boy! woa then! Theer's a smock-frock and ould hat a-hangin up, might come in useful.

G. F. And a bridle with a knot of orange-tawny ribbon:—A puritan household—hm.—Yet for the present we must lie in the frying-pan rather than jump into the fire. Here's the King's Majesty's letter: where best to hide it?

Tom. Your honour's boot.

G. F. First place people search.

Tom. Your hat might——

G. F. Fly away any moment.

Tom. The bandage.   [*Points to wounded arm.*

G. F. Hm, 'twill need dressing, and who will the chirurgeon be?

Tom. It ought a' been a-looked-to ere now. Could I tie theas letter under your honour's hair? No one 'ood catch a glimpse o't. (*Action in accordance.—Shouts outside.*) What's that? Zome-one at gate?

G. F. (*Listens.*) They're passing on. They're gone by. No, Tom (*takes out his purse*), I'll put it here.

Tom. Very first place, *I* should zay, to be ran-sackt.

G. F. By Goring's men or Wilmot's; as well fall in with a gang of highwaymen. The Roundheads are no pickpockets.

Tom. (*Listening, and pointing thumb over shoulder into stable, whispers.*) Zir, a noise within.

G. F. (*Looks*). Only the rightful tenant twitching his halter. See how much is in it.

[*Hands purse to* Tom.

Tom. Sixteen jacōbuses, and zilver to boot, zir.

G. F. Clap the silver in thy poke—so! Hand me out six gold pieces—so! (*Pockets them.*) Among the remainder (*takes purse*) this cypher must lie, folded small,—with which make thou all speed to his Royal Highness at Exeter or elsewhere, should Fortune my foe force me to give the charge to thee. Suppose us taken, and they consent to enlarge thee, as is often done with those of lesser note, I toss thee this purse to clear wages and so forth, and thou must put it up and vanish.

Tom. 'Ithout the smallest delay, zir. But I hope your honour 'ill do your own arrands.

G. F. You'll find your way to Devon?

Tom. Like a carrier-pigeon to 's cote. But soft! zomebody's a-comin'.

G. F. Stand in!

[*Draws sword with left hand.* Tom *takes up the axe. They go into stable, softly shutting the door after them.*

Enter from house (C) Naomi Radclyffe.

Naomi. I must look after poor Lightfoot myself; with things in this confusion they might forget to feed her. Jerry!—O where is this foolish groom? Jerry! (*opens stable door.*) Lightfoot, then! Wo-ho, lass!

[*Makes a step forward and sees the intruders; steps backward in alarm, her eyes fixed on the doorway, at which now appear* Fortescue *and* Tom *behind him. The former sheathes his sword and salutes her respectfully.*

G. F. Madam—

N. (*Quickly and with dignity.*)   What are you, sir?

G. F.   A wounded man, madam, and it may be a prisoner.

N.   A prisoner?

G. F.   At your mercy, madam, if you choose to give us up.

N.   Who is this other man?

G. F.   My servant, madam.

Tom.   Only Tom Trivet, mistress, late of North Devon, where he would fain be again.

N.   And *your* name, sir?

G. F.   George Fortescue, madam.

N.   You are of the King's army. (*Aside.*)   Is nobody coming?

G. F.   Yes, madam.

Tom.   —While he had one.

N.   My father by affection and honour is bound to the other side, and his household and neighbours are staunch for the Parliament.

Tom. (*Whispers.*) Shall I vling my cloak o'er her head?

G. F. (*Indignantly, but in undertone.*)   Silence!— Madam—(*makes as though he would come forward.*)

N.   Sir, move not hand or foot, I caution you! Will you force me to raise my voice?   (*Aside.*) Would I could hear anyone stirring!

G. F.   We would not, madam, offend you in the least particular.

N.   Do you yield yourself?

G. F.   Pardon me, madam; that I will not do, save in extremity.

N.   There is no harbour for you here.   You must surrender (*he makes a negative gesture*) or else— (*Aside.*)   There's not a soul left about the house!

G. F.   Or else?

N.   Go through that gate, by which you have entered.   I will not hinder you.

G. F.   That were to be made prisoners immediately.

N. You must choose, and quickly. (*Aside.*) I cannot hold up much longer!

G. F. Hear me one moment, madam. You perhaps have some who are dear to you engaged in the war. (NAOMI *sighs; he watches her face.*) They also may be in peril—wounded—in need of compassion.

N. What would you ask, sir?

G. F. That you suffer us to rest in the corner of this stable until dusk, and then glide off like ghosts or shadows, if we have luck enough.

N. I know not if I may rightly do this.

G. F. Ask your own heart, which I am sure is not without pity for the unfortunate.

N. Are you much hurt, sir?

G. F. Not much, I thank you, lady.

Tom. Enow, by George, for one turn!

G. F. A little surgery will set all right.

Tom. Heaven zend it may!

N. I would we could help you better. Is there a bullet in your arm, sir?

G. F. A pistol bullet, fair lady,—from one of our own men, too, by Jupiter!

N. Your own men?—traitors?

G. F. Not so.

N. How then could it chance?

G. F. Will you care to hear? The battle well-nigh over, in a sudden encounter of two bodies of horse I rode across one of our men's pistols, just as he gave fire, and down I came.

Tom. But your honour doesn't tell all. He rode forward thus hastily, madam, to zave a Roundhead Officer (begging your pardon) in bad case enow, dismounted, tangled wi' his wounded hoss, his steel cap off; but still he wa-ived his sword and shouted to 's men. You lizzen, lady?

N. I do indeed.

Tom. Well—two of our troopers in vury o' battle

rides at 'en vull butt—my measter here roars to hold
hard—no use—spurs in at zame instant, jist in time
to zave th' oul' fella and catch a bullet in's own sword-
arm.

N. Doth the wound bleed?

G. F. Not now, madam. Tom here, tho' he had
a fall in the same melée, bandaged me cleverly.

Tom. Lord be praised I weren't far off.

N. And this officer whose life you saved?

G. F. Both sides drew off—I saw or heard no more
of him.

N. 'Twas a good deed, sir; and on this, if no other
argument, I'll make bold to give you harbour till
evening. You can lock this door inside, and I will
take order that none troubles you. You shall have
meat and drink, and the wicket unbolted for your
exit—at what hour?

G. F. At eleven, madam, so please you.

N. At eleven. Take this key. And now, fare you
well, and may God keep you both.

G. F. Farewell, madam—my heart thanks you, and
while it beats, your kind and sweet compassion shall
never be forgotten. One word more—may I crave
your name?

N. Naomi Radclyffe.

G. F. Once heard and for ever; no need to write
it down. Madam, farewell!

   [*She bows and moves away; he says in undertone.*
Fain had I sued for leave to kiss her hand;
But that were too much daring. What are all
The beauties of the Court compared with her?

      [*She glances round.*
Farewell!—and she is gone, perhaps for ever.

   [*Loud knocking and calling heard at the gate;
    a body of Parliament troopers are want-
    ing to come in. FORTESCUE and TOM at
    stable door listening. NAOMI, almost
    off, turns and comes back hastily.*

N. In, and lock the door!

G. F. But—

N. In at once!   [*They go in; clamour at gate increases.*

Voices outside. Hillo within!—Open quickly!—Open to the Parliament!—Burst it in, without more parley!

N. Hold! Who is there?

Voice. Do you speak at last? Open to General Fairfax's men, and speedily.

N. Your name, sir?

Voice. Captain Radclyffe, in command of a party of horse.

N. Charlton's voice. (*Opens wicket.*) This way, cousin. The great gate is fast, and I cannot undo it.

Enter Captain CHARLTON RADCLYFFE.

Charlton. Ha—you, Cousin Naomi! Where are all your folk?

N. None here, through the confusions of the time and hour. I am sorry you have had to wait. (*Earnestly.*) What news bring you, cousin?

Ch. Victory, cousin, is our news—and a great one. You have seen none of the fugitives, I suppose?

N. I have not been abroad to-day. Have you any news of my father?

Ch. I am expecting it, and good, please Heaven, at every instant. Have you been long in the stable-yard?

N. Not long. I but came to see that my mare starve not in the general disorder. *Where* is my father?

Ch. I know not precisely where; we were separated. But with your leave, cousin. (*Calls.*) Corporal Grome! Attention! The men I name will dismount and come in here; nearest left-hand men to hold the horses. The rest keep their posts. Hardy!

Hardy. Here, sir!

[*Soldiers answer and step through
wicket in turn.*

Ch. Hezekiah Wood!

Here, sir.

Carstairs!

Here, sir.

Freeman!

Here, sir.

Watch-and-Pray Dobson!

Here, sir.

Form line—steady!

N. (*Anxiously.*) Intend you quartering with us to-night, cousin?

Ch. We may trouble you, cousin. Room here for a score of men and horses, and goodwill, I know. How doth mine honoured aunt? I ought to have asked sooner. We'll take up no quarters till her good leave be granted.

N. My mother is ill at ease, as you may well guess. But cousin, cousin, will you not say if you know aught of my father? Is some dreadful thing hid behind this curtain of silence?

Ch. No, in good sooth, cousin. We rode separate ways. I am now, understand, in hot pursuit of certain fugitives of the King's army, especially one young man of rank, of Rupert's regiment, suspected as bearer of a despatch for the malignants in the West. He, with one that by description is his servant, must be in some hiding-place not far off, and it seemed better that I should search here than a stranger. So, with your leave, fair cousin, we'll lose no more time, knowing you will rejoice as much as any if these sons of Belial can be seized. Now, men, bustle round; search the stables and outhouses! Find the rats! Our terriers watch outside, if they slip through.

Enter Servants—PRUDENCE, JERUSHA, JERRY, OLD
CROOKES—*who talk confusedly to each other.*

Mercy on us!—Heaven protect us!—What do they
in our place?—Here's our young lady!—How is't
madam?
                    [*The soldiers search the stable-yard.*
N. (*To* CHARLTON.) You are certain my father is
safe?
Ch. As sure as trusty information can make me.
But, Naomi,—
N. (*Alarmed.*) What?
Ch. You have never asked a word touching your
cousin's well-being.
N. Cousin—what cousin?
Ch. (*Bowing.*) Your servant—now and always.
N. Nay, cousin, I see thee safe and well.
Ch. I might be wounded, for all that—but I am
not; or have escaped by a hair's breadth,—which I
did; but you care not.
N. I am glad you are safe.
Ch. I thank you.
                    [*The soldiers come to door of small
                        stable and try it.*
Trooper. This is locked.
N. That is where my mare is lodged.
Ch. Where's the key?
N. You'll frighten Lightfoot; she's mettlesome
and nervous.
Ch. Nay; we'll take measures with her. Let me
have the key.
N. I have it not.
Ch. (*To servants.*) One of you find it. Quick!
Servants. 'Tis not with me.
                    —I know not where 'tis.
                    —Do'st know, Jerry?
                    —Not I, good sooth!

Ch. (*To* NAOMI.) Can't you think where it may be found?

N. What need your men go in there It is my stable, and locked.

Jerusha. Could one get through keyhole—save a witch?

Ch. (*In undertone to* NAOMI.) Your pardon, Naomi, but I must search this place thoroughly. Why tease me thus? 'Tis no time for thine old girlish tricks

N. I gave them up long ago, I hope, cousin.

Corporal Grome. (*Coming forward*). The men have searched all round, sir, and stand idle.

Ch. Prise open the door with as little force as will serve.

Corporal. (*To* CHARLTON.) Sir, the prudent man, saith Solomon, looketh well to his going. Let us use caution.

[*The men are ranged on each side of door with swords drawn.* CHARLTON *draws pistol from his belt and looks to the priming. Two soldiers force the door open. A pause.*

Ch. Corporal Grome—Hezekiah Wood—guard the door. The rest go in.

[*Men go into stable.*

'Twill not take long to search.

Grome. (*Looking in.*) There's a loft, sir.

[*The soldiers reappear.*

Ch. Well?

Soldier. Nothing, sir, but a trim little bay nag.

Another. (*Rubbing his leg.*) Gave me a taste of her hoof, and beshrew her!

Jerusha. Used you properly!

Naomi. Prudence, ask my mother to come hither at once, but alarm her not. Say there's no ill news.

[*Exit* PRUDENCE.

Ch. You tried the loft, too?

Soldier. Ay, sir; there's nobody.

8

Jerry. (*Aside to* JERUSHA.) If there had a been somebody, he were true idiot not to find the little window at back.

Soldier (*who has been looking round corner*). Sir, there's a little window at the back, unbolted, and footmarks in the midden without.

Ch. Corporal, see that the men outside are on the alert. Hardy, Watch-and-Pray Dobson, stay with me; the rest, off. Search every cranny!

[*After a pause* GEORGE FORTESCUE *is brought in, disarmed and angry.*

G. F. Stand off, fellows! You have my sword.

Ch. Made he resistance?

Corporal. So far as a hurt man could.

[FORTESCUE *groans involuntarily.*

Ch. What ails you, sir?

N. See you not he is wounded?

G. F. My arm is somewhat painful, sir.

Ch. Press not on him. Who are you, sir?

G. F. I do not choose to answer.

Ch. Then I'll tell you: George Fortescue, second son of the late Lord Lyndore, of the county of Devon; and now on a secret errand of treasonable purport.

G. F. (*Scornfully.*) Treasonable!

Ch. Ay, sir. The King being in the hands of evil counsellors and Popish traitors who misadvise him, against the true interest of crown and kingdom.

G. F. Pshaw, sir! one has heard this stuff too often.

(*Apart.*)
N. (*To* JERUSHA.) Is my mother coming, think you?

J. Prudence would lose no time, madam.

N. May Heaven help us!

Ch. What say you, Naomi?

N. Nothing.

Corporal. (*Sententiously, after clearing his throat.*) We have our warrant; yea, the Gospel light shineth in

our inward parts. We fight against the Antichrist,
and all Popish, prelatical, malignant men!

Hezekiah Wood. (*With a strong twang.*) Wherefore
the Lord will save us from the curse of Meroz, who
would not help the Lord against the mighty.

Corporal. Silence in the ranks!

Ch. Enough, both of you! (*To* FORTESCUE.) We
defend the true rights of the Nation and the King.

G. F. I'll tell you what you are—a swarm of fools,
Set on by cunning and malicious knaves!
Helping a rebel rabble parliament
To wreck the ancient fabric of this realm
Because a stone or two is out of place;
To break the Crown, which caps and keeps together
Th' ascending cone of dignities and duties,
And let all rush to ruin!

Ch. Come, no more, sir!

J. (*To* NAOMI.) He speaks foinely, don't he?

N. Alas! how will this end?

G. F. Soldiers! your sires were honest folk, content
To fear God, honour the King, and live in peace
And plenty with each other. Are you wiser?
England flung topsy-turvy, will that serve you?

Ch. Peace, you were best!

G. F. Rogues flourish in such times, not honest men,
And by-and-by, when retribution comes,
You all will feel it, and your children too!

Ch. (*Raising his pistol.*) Silence him!

[*Soldiers surround* FORTESCUE.

N. Merciful Heaven!

G. F. (*Stepping free of them for a moment.*) Come,
friends! your lawful King will pardon you. Who's
for King Charles?

Ch. (*Cocking and presenting pistol.*) Nay, if you will
not.

N. (*Shrieks and rushes forward.*) Do not fire. He's
weaponless and wounded.

8—2

Ch. This is no business for thee, Naomi Radclyffe.

Enter Mistress RADCLYFFE.

N. It is for *her.* O mother, thou art come at last!

Mistr. R. Charlton Radclyffe!—nephew!—what may this mean?

Ch. My humble service to you, gracious aunt.

Mistr. R. What of my husband? Know you where Colonel Radclyffe is, and how?

Ch. For the present, no, madam; but I am momently expecting news.

Mistr. R. Poor comfort!

Ch. No cause for dread, my dear aunt. But pardon, gracious madam, my duty waits. Corporal, look to your prisoner. See that he makes away with no paper. He must be searched.

G. F. (*Aside.*) You are too late!

Ch. If he talks again—the gag!

N. Mother, you will save him?

Mistr. R. Your prisoner—permit me. Sir, who and what are you?

G. F. My name is Fortescue, madam.

Mistr. R. And your baptized name?

G. F. George, madam.

Mistr. R. George Fortescue,—are you of Devon?

G. F. That is my county, madam.

Mistr. Son of the good Lord Lyndore?

G. F. You know my father's name?

N. (*To her mother.*) O madam! you know this gentleman's kin? You will plead for him?

Mistr. R. I knew your mother, sir, when both of us were girls, and loved her. Yes, Naomi; you have heard me speak of Philippa Chenies, of Moreton—that was she. I am very sorry, sir, trust me, to see you in my house on such unhappy terms. Your hurts must be looked to. Nephew, *I* will be warrant for your prisoner's safe keeping.

N. This will certainly suffice you?

Ch. Good, my aunt and cousin, I may not lose sight of him. He has, most likely, papers of consequence about him.

G. F. None, upon my honour, sir.

N. You do not doubt his word?

Mistr. R. Come, come, nephew, let him be brought in. Am not I Colonel Radclyffe's wife? I'll have a chamber made ready. Come with me, Prudence. Naomi, look to Mr. Fortescue meanwhile.

[*Exit Mistress* RADCLYFFE.

N. Charlton, you will yield to my mother in this?

Ch. I must not, Naomi.

N. Nay—surely . . .

Enter three troopers, bringing TOM *a prisoner, disguised in a smock frock and old hat.*

Ch. Who's here?

Trooper. We took this fellow, sir, in the mown meadow hard by, squatting in the hedge like a hare.

Ch. What is he?

Trooper. A countryman he says. (*Snatches* TOM's *hat off.*) You, sir, speak up for yourself!

Tom. (*Hesitatingly.*) Plaise your honour, I'm a poor innocent lad——

Jerry. (*Coming forward.*) You're a rogue, a rogue, that's what you are! Why he's a-got my owd frock on, and that there 'at's my 'at and norne else's!

Ch. Uncase him!

[*They pull smock over* TOM's *ears and show him in military dress.*

Tom. (*Sulkily.*) Dowl! don't pull a chap to pieces!

Ch. (*Meanwhile, in undertone to* NAOMI.) Naomi, how came they in thy stable?

N. By their own act.

Ch. Wholly?

Trooper. (*Snatching a purse out of* TOM's *pocket.*) Look'ee here!

Tom. What, are ye cutpurses too?

G. F. (*To* CHARLTON.) Your pardon, sir; this I own is my man, who hath in vain attempted to escape, and the purse is mine.

Tom. The purse is my master's.

Ch. Take it, sir. (*Is handing it to* FORTESCUE, *when* GROME *interposes.*)

Grome. With favour, Captain—the counsels of the wicked are deceit.

Ch. Thy meaning?

Grome. Let the purse be opened; yea, let the secrets thereof be brought to light.

> [CHARLTON *opens purse and finds paper, which he unfolds and examines.*

Ch. Cypher. It must to head-quarters at once, with both prisoners.

N. You will wait till my mother returns?

Ch. Not another instant!

> [*Troopers seize* FORTESCUE *roughly; he pushes them aside;* CHARLTON *steps forward.*

Will you not go quietly?

G. F. (*Staggering.*) Your pardon, sir, . . . I was wrong, I own . . . but . . .

> [*He faints;* TOM *rushes forward and raises him;* NAOMI *helps;* CHARLTON *comes near and looks at* FORTESCUE; *says contemptuously—*

Ch. Pshaw, this is nothing! Remove him!

> [NAOMI *turns to* CHARLTON.

N. Charlton Radclyffe, stand back, and your men too! We will not suffer this—not for fifty Parliaments! The son of my mother's old friend—wounded —worn out—dying perhaps! If you lay hands on him you must on me too. This is my father's house—my mother will be answerable for him before God and man—and stir he shall not, till he hath been duly cared for and is fit to move !

[*The soldiers look at each other ;* CHARL-
TON *undetermined and much vexed.*

Ch. Is it thus *you* speak, Naomi?

N. Even thus ! Here (*to servants*), see to the gentleman ; (TOM *helps*) lift him, gently—now in !

Ch. (*Coming close to her.*)   One word, Naomi !

N. (*Pushing past him.*)   Not one !   Be tender with
his hurt arm.   He revives, I think.   Sir, you are with
friends, and shall want for no care Ashby Manor can
give you.

Ch. (*To soldiers.*)   Follow, but hold back a little.

[FORTESCUE *is supported towards
the house.*

Enter Mistress RADCLYFFE (C) *meeting them.*

Mistr. R. All is ready.

Ch. He shall not stay in this house !

END OF SCENE I.

SCENE II.

*A Room in the Manor House, panelled ; with sober, ancient
furniture.*

Enter Mistress RADCLYFFE, *speaking.*

Mistr. R. Prudence !

Enter PRUDENCE.

Let him on no excuse be disturbed.

P. No, madam.   [*Exit.*

Mistr. R. (Alone.) My private grief comes back—
    grows worse each hour.
Ah, dreadful days! when fellow-countrymen,
Companions, neighbours, friends, stand opposite
With deadly and implacable resolve
To deluge English soil with English blood!
Thou God of Battles! be my husband's guard!
His cause is Thy cause: Thou wilt keep Thy chosen.
—And if he should be slain? Good men have fall'n.
                                 [Sits down.
Ay, many a new-made widow now in England,
And many an orphan. Daughter! what were we
In this rude world without thy father's face?
Basil, come back to us! come back to us!
He hears not.   Shall we ever have again
The sweet old quiet times? One other week
Brings round the longest day: O month of June!—
That golden June in my dear Devon once!
The honeysuckle-scented summer nights,
Warm stars and whispering wind among the leaves,
More loud than lovers' voices,—yet we miss'd
No word each other spoke. How well I knew
His horse's gallop on the little bridge
And up the lane; then came the light, quick step,
The tender word, and I was in his arms.
My Sweetheart! One of such a constant mind
As when my flush of youth and beauty waned
His fondness but increased; in England's realm
No woman warmlier loved, no wife more honour'd.
And now—*his* life flung out into the whirl
Of a bloody tempest, scattering death and torture!
                                 [Starts up
O senseless fool! weak wailing coward! *[Rings a bell.*

       Enter woman.

                Quick!
Is there a horse left? Someone saddle him,

This moment—ay, for *me*—haste, haste, I say!
I'll follow.   [*Exit woman, bewildered.*

Enter NAOMI.

N. Whither go you, dearest mother?
Mistr. R. To the battle-field.
N. The battle-field! What to do there?
Mistr. R. Search for him.
N. What fear you? 'Tis impossible! His men
who love him, General Fairfax who honours him,
would never—— O, mother, news may come at any
moment!
Mistr. R. I must go.
N. If he himself returned and found us gone.
Mistr. R. You are not wont to disobey me, Naomi;
I thought you loved your father.
N. O dearest mother, we will go together!
You are right—and walk if need be.
                    [*Raises her mother and supports her
                         towards the door* (L).
Come, sweet mother, we'll soon get ready.

Enter servant woman (L).

Servant. Master Charlton, madam, craves leave to
speak with you.
Mistr. R. Let him enter.
                    [*Servant bows, goes out, and returns, showing
                         in* CHARLTON. (L.)
Mistr. R. Have you news?
Ch. None, madam, I—
Mistr. R. (*Not noticing his intention to speak on.*)
We have been distant, nephew, for some years. Let
the storm press us closer. I am heartily sorry to give

you so poor a welcome. And now urgent business calls us from home immediately.

Ch. From home, madam,—on such a day as this?—and whither?

N. To the battle-field.

Ch. Mere madness to think of it! the country swarming with wild, disorderly soldiers, fevered with victory, frantic with defeat,—

Mistr. R. God will protect us.

Ch. Madam, you must not think of this. I will not, with all respect, suffer it.

Mistr. R. How say you?

N. Not suffer!—sir, you presume somewhat far on your relationship—or is it your military rank makes you an intermeddler?

Ch. (*Smiling.*) Be satisfied, fair cousin; I understand these matters; and once for all—it may not be.

N. Will you stay us by force?

Ch. You will not put me to it. I act but for your good, believe it.

> [*Mistress* RADCLYFFE *sinks into a chair exhausted.*

N. Poor mother! (*Turns to* CHARLTON.) You saw nothing of my father after mid-day?

Ch. Nothing, fair cousin, but I doubt not he is safe.

Mistr. R. (*Rousing herself.*) Why say you so?

Ch. Well (*hesitating*), 'tis a little strange, perhaps, we should not have heard ere this.

Mistr. R. Strange, indeed! Charlton, you believe he's killed? I see it in your face. O nephew, nephew, how could you leave the field, his fate in balance? You loved him not—you were ever cold-hearted!

Ch. Nay, madam—

N. Mother, mother!

> [*Mistress* R. *collects herself.*

Ch. Madam, I came to say a word, with your permission, touching my prisoner, Lord Lyndore.

Mistr. R. George Fortescue, you mean ; Lord Lyndore is his elder brother.

Ch. *Was*, madam. This is a time of sudden heritages. *He*, I have just learnt, lies cold on Naseby field ; and my prisoner is Lord Lyndore, a man of consequence, head of his family : besides which, he is bearer from the King of private orders for the West. His arm is now bandaged they tell me. I must carry him to General Fairfax.

N. He is not fit to travel.

Ch. Did *you* dress his arm ?

N. I gave my help. The bullet is still in, and he cannot ride.

Ch. We'll tie him on.

Mistr. R. Nephew, you *must not* use this young man harshly.

Ch. Aunt, he shall be used as well as haste and these rough times allow.

N. Charlton, you will not drag him off?

Ch. By no means, fair cousin ; but he must come quietly, and without more delay. Your pardon, madam, —(*going*).

Mistr. R. Stop, Charlton ! I have pledged my word for his safe custody. Let him stay for the present in our keeping.

Ch. I may not, aunt ; and the more because you *are* my aunt, to make myself suspect of favour. Pray you, say no more. I humbly take my leave. Farewell. Farewell, sweet cousin. (*Aside to her.*) I would speak with you on a grave business before I go—a few words.

N. (*Aside to him.*) I'll see my mother in and return hither. (*Aloud.*) Come, mother, you were best lie down awhile.

Mistr. R. My head whirls. I know not what to do.

N. Lean on me, mother.   [*Exeunt together* (*R*).

[CHARLTON *stays, opens door* (*L*), *and whistles, not loud.*

Enter GROME.

Ch. Shut the door. Thou rememberest where
and when chance first threw thee in my way?—and
why I have taken thee into the regiment at no small
risk?

Grome. Very well, sir.

Ch. Never forget it. I have more work for thee.
Play me fair, it shall profit thee well. Go about to
trick me, and—thou knowest what I am.

Grome. Ay, sir, ever since—

Ch. (*Interrupting.*) And what *thou* art.

Grome. Your dog, sir; my hopes and aims follow
humbly at heel of yours.

Ch. My uncle may be among the slain.

Grome. I'm sure on't. That would change your
honour's plans?

Ch. Help them on. Who saw him fall?

Grome. Three several men told me.

Ch. (*Chiefly to himself.*) There has not been time to
sort the dead. The messengers may come at any moment with this news. And then how stand I? What
shall I be then?

Grome. Lifted, sir, I humbly hope, as on the wings
of the morning, out of the valley of debt and despondency.

Ch. Pshaw!—He was a good man, so all say.
Jealous of me, after Providence decreed the death of
my young cousin, and left me heir presumptive.

Grome. A fine estate, sir.

Ch. A small thing. In any case I shall make excuse
to leave thee behind me here. Thou wilt watch how
things go,—and be *safer* here, for the present.

Grome. (*Murmurs.*) Your honour is too kind to
me.

Ch. This inheritance would scarce clear my credit.

I shall win the larger stake—and thou shalt profit.
But remember, 'tis a dangerous game.
 Grome. I'll do my little part, sir, I hope.
     [*Sound of door shutting in corridor.*
Ch. Some one comes—Go—but wait within call.
Grome. I will, sir.
Ch. And let the men be ready.
Grome. Yes, sir.   [*Exit.*
Ch. I trust him, with a pistol to his ear.
My dog, yes—one, too, that could show his teeth:
So far he has fetch'd and carried very neatly.
 How often little Naomi and I
Play'd hide and seek in these old corridors!
Pest on these family quarrels! Was't my fault
My baby cousin died? Now is the time
To make all round and smooth. She's hot of temper,
But readily appeased; and, for the rest,
A woman,—ay, the fairest in seven shires!
I am, or shall be, and perhaps I am
Lord of this manor. Naomi and my aunt
Will sorely need protection; who but I
Through natural duty should afford it them?
But not a word of love—beware of that!—
Until my plans are riper—

Enter NAOMI.

      Ah, sweet cousin!
 N. What would you, cousin? I have but a moment
to stay.
 Ch. Time was, Naomi, you were ready enough to
keep me company, play, run, read, whisper,—kiss me
too.
 N. When we were children.
 Ch. Is there no memory of kindness left? Cousin,
I would crave your friendly ear for some discourse that
much concerns us both.

N. I listen; but I must pray you to be brief.

Ch. Your father—

N. What would you tell me?

Ch. Nay, nothing more than hath been told already.
But this time may be a fit one, among close kin as we
are, to recon the map and roadbook of our family life:
no future but must continuate the past.

N. What aim you at?

Ch. This. You know, doubtless, fair cousin, that I
am next heir to this estate. And you cannot but have
heard also of my grandfather's dying wish, that should
your father have no son to inherit, you, his only
daughter, and myself, when years were ripe, might if
possible be wedded.

N. I *have* heard this,—but never liked it.

Ch. Would that were otherwise! But if't be so,
So be it.   Yet remember, at the least,
I am your cousin; and if changeful fortune
Bring such a need, a lamentable need,
This house, dear Naomi, will still be yours—
Your mother's—in all dignity and honour.

N. How mean you?

Ch.   Ashby Manor is your home,
Whatever happens.

N.   Were my father gone,—
Is that your meaning?

Ch. (*With pauses.*)   Yes, dear Naomi.—
You know me not—indeed you know me not.
Will you not speak? Is not the offer worth
A word of answer?

N. (*Absently.*) O, I thank you, cousin,
I thank you—but my thoughts were otherwhere.

Ch. And you accept? Say merely you accept.

N. Charlton, my mother and myself would leave
This house for ever, were my father gone!

Ch. But wherefore?—why should this be, Naomi?
We used to live in kindlier confidence—

'Twas chance that sunder'd us, not wrath or reason.
Will you not let me even be your friend?
And whither would my aunt go?   Into Devon?
I pray you, answer me.
   N.   You speak as tho'
My father were already lost to us.
   Ch. Naomi, in sad truth, I fear he is.
   N. You fear that?   Do you know it?—But you
       fear it?
O Heaven have pity!
   Ch.   Naomi—
   N.   No more!
   Ch. Nay, go not!—hear me!—say you hate me not?
What have I done that you should use me thus?
   N. Cousin, I hate not, and did never hate you.
Again I thank you.   Pray you, let me pass.
   Ch. Naomi—I love thee! dost thou hear?—I love
       thee,
Love none but thee—have loved thee all these years—
Have set my heart and soul on winning thee!—
Why should I have no chance to win thy love?
Am I not manly enough to look upon?
Hast ever heard them call me coward?—Nay
You do me wrong by this cold, cruel bearing!
Will you not speak—not even listen to me?
                   [*She turns away.*
You must!—you shall not go yet!
            [*Seizes her arm; she shrieks.*
                Naomi!
Would'st drive me mad?

Enter LYNDORE, *without armour or sword, his arm*
         bandaged.

   Lyn. Stand back, sir! what do you with this lady
   Ch. How, sir, come you here?
   Lyn. For this lady's protection, if she need it.
   Ch. She needs it not.

Lyn. I will not take your word for that. Madam, forgive me ; I heard your voice raised as in sudden fear.

Ch. Where were your sentries?

Lyn. (*Not heeding him.*) Nay, you shrieked.

Ch. I'll trounce the careless knaves !

N. (*To* LYNDORE.) I truly thank you, sir. Something told hastily by my cousin startled me ; but all is now settled.

Ch. (*To* LYNDORE.) My Lord Lyndore, back to ward !

Lyn. Jackanapes !

Ch. Insolent.   [*Half draws his sword.*

N. (*To* CHARLTON.) Upon a wounded man ! Hold, for shame ! (*To* LYNDORE.) I pray you !

Ch. (*To* LYNDORE.) Know me better, Lord Lyndore. I am master here ; nay, doubly, triply master. I am this lady's cousin—

Lyn. But not her master.

Ch. After Colonel Radclyffe, I am head of this family ; and further, in present command of a troop of—

Lyn. Rascal rebels !

Ch. No more words !   [*Opens door and calls*] Grome !

Grome. (*Without.*) Here, sir.

Ch. Where are your men ?

Grome. This way, men. [GROME *and soldiers enter.*

Ch. Take your prisoner, and look better to him. Prepare to mount immediately. Strap him to Carstairs if needful. Ready !

    [*Soldiers surround Lord* LYNDORE. *Enter Mistress* RADCLYFFE *and servants.*

N. O mother !

Mistr. R. Nephew, will you do yourself and our house this dishonour?

Ch. Dishonour?—He must go, madam aunt,—your pardon, but he must.

N. Madam, will you suffer it ?

9

Servant-woman. Truly, 'twill be his death!

Ch. Men, remove the prisoner!

Mistr. R. Stir not, I command you!

Ch. On!

> [*The soldiers prepare to remove Lord* LYNDORE, *and* CHARLTON *to follow, when a side-door opens, and Colonel* RADCLYFFE *steps in. He is in military dress, soiled, and without a sword. All silent and amazed for a moment or two.*

Col. R. Hey! what's to do here?

Mistr. R. O Basil! (*Embracing him.*) Is it thou indeed?

N. Father!   [*Clasps him and kisses his hands.*

Col. R. Truly, sweethearts, I am no ghost or goblin, —though fain to creep in thus.

Mistr. R. And you are safe?

Col. R. And sound, through Heaven's mercy. Thus it was, wife: my horse shot and I prisoner, carried mounted towards Rugby, my captors were set upon by some of our side, and in the confusion I galloped off. Two or three pistol shots followed me, but no harm done,—and here I am.

Servants. (The good Heavens be praised! / God bless your honour!

Col. R. But what business is toward? Who are these gentlemen? Eh,—Charlton?

Ch. Mine honoured uncle. I heartily rejoice to see you safe in your own good house.

Col. R. I thank thee as heartily, nephew. Now, explain.

Ch. I was sent hither by Colonel Hammond in pursuit of fugitives, and have taken Lord Lyndore with a letter in cypher—whom I am even now at point of removing to General Fairfax's quarters at Market-Harborough.

Mistr. R. (*In undertone.*) Dear husband, the gentleman is wounded and unfit to move.

Col. R. Let me see the prisoner. [CHARLTON *motions to soldiers, who bring forward Lord* LYNDORE. Are you Lord Lyndore?

Lyn. So I hear, sir, to my great grief.

Col. R. You have been wounded in the fight?

Lyn. In the arm, sir.

Col. R. (*Interested and coming near.*) In the arm! Ha, stay! 'twas a pistol-shot, I think?—at close quarters?—which you received in protecting an officer of the enemy dismounted and sore beset? Yes, yes! —I pray you look me in the face.

Lyn. I seem to know your face, sir.

Col. R. You *do!* Look again! Look at me well! Wife!—daughter!—this brave young gentleman gave me my life at peril of his own. That wound he took for *me.* How shall he be thanked?

Mistr. R. With all we have and are!

N. May God bless you!

Lyn. You have already repaid me richly. [*A scuffle at door:* TOM's *voice heard*—" *Ye sha'n't stop me!*"— Is that my man?

Tom (*Bursting through soldiers.*) 'Tes, Measter George! (*kneels and kisses his hand*)—and where your honour stays I'll stay, dead or alive!

[*Soldiers make as though to take* TOM.

Col. R. Leave him alone. He shall wait on his master.

Tom. God bless your noble honour!

Ch. (*Aside.*) The blue plague seize them! (*Aloud, sullenly.*) What orders, sir?

Col. R. Half of the men remain here for the present. You with the rest ride to General Fairfax, give him the paper you have taken, and say I follow quickly.

Mistr. R. Go so soon!

Col. R. Yes, dear. I came but to assure you of my safety, and must back to duty.

N. And when will you come to us again?

Col. R. Soon, darling: soon I hope—and to stay.

Ch. The prisoners, Colonel Radclyffe?

Col. R. I charge myself with them. Draw off half your men and mount. Farewell. Barrett!

Trooper. Here, Colonel.

Col. R. Ride for the chirurgeon; you'll find him at Hinckley Farm, bring him hither as soon as may be. Take a second horse. Quick! (*To* CHARLTON, *who lingers*). How now?

Ch. With your favour, sir, I conceive it my duty to carry my prisoners to the General.

Col. R. With your favour, sir, conceive it your first duty to obey your superior officer. I have not lost my colonelcy on the road. To horse, sir, with no more delay!

Ch. I obey, sir. I meant to leave the Corporal (*indicates* GROME) with a man or two for the protection of the house.

Col. R. I will see to that.

Ch. (*Going—mutters.*) They shall all rue this! *She among the rest.*   [*Exit.*

N. O Father, thank Heaven you are safe!

Mistr. R. And this gentleman its chosen instrument!

(*Col. R. To Lord* LYNDORE.) My lord, I owe you an arm. Come.

Mistr. R. (*As they go.*) Prudence!—Martha!—the south chamber! See after them, Naomi.

N. Yes, dear mother!

> [*Colonel and Mistress* RADCLYFFE *help Lord* LYNDORE (R.) NAOMI *stands for a moment near door* (L) *watching them off with a look of joy. She clasps her hands, raises her eyes, and exclaims fervently,* "*Thank Heaven!*" *then exit quickly.*
>
> GROME, *standing stiffly as on duty, is seen watching all the proceedings; he changes his attitude and looks keenly after* NAOMI *while Drop falls.*

 END OF ACT I.

ACT II.—SCENE I.

[*Three months later. Large Chamber or Anteroom of the Manor
House, ground floor, half sitting-room, half hall : practicable
door at back, open ; large Tudor windows, the casements open ;
giving upon a Terrace, beyond which stretches an autumnal
landscape. Practicable doors, R side 1st E, L side 3rd E.*

*Music between Acts 1 and 2 of a sweet and peaceful character ;
founded on, or including, airs of the period ; it continues after
the curtain rises.*

The scene is for a moment or two empty, then NAOMI *and Lord* LYN-
DORE *are seen slowly passing the window in conversation, and
presently enter, as from a walk : the music dying away as they
come in. He wears a wide Cavalier hat with plume, and a
simple but handsome dress. She has in her hand some wild
flowers and ears of corn. He takes off his hat on entering. He
is pale and thin, but his arm is no longer tied up.*]

N. A glorious autumn day !

Lyn.   The whole rich world
Basks like a mellow apple in the sun.
That corn was green when first I cross'd your bounds
A fugitive,—now, amber head to head,
Nodding and whispering as peacefully
As if no hostile camp or battle-field
Scored England's face with ugly frowns and scars.

                    [*Looks at corn and flowers which she holds.*
Lady, the summer sun that ripen'd these
Beat heavily upon my fever'd brain.
How I have tried your patience ! burthen'd all
Your household with my sickness !

N.   Who that breathes
Could aid, and would not ?—When, at last, your fever
Sunk into heavy sleep, a vestibule
Of solemn darkness, with two opposite doors,

To life, to death, and, so God will'd, at last
The door of life unfolded,—what reward
For us the watchers, to see *your* sane eyes
Look out with recognition!

 Lyn.   Not at first
I saw who sat and watch'd me ; but it seem'd
Continuation of a dream of Heav'n.
Then flow'd assurance in, it was indeed
No visionary angel, and for once
Dream was outvied by the reality.
—Will you not rest?
      [*She sits down and puts off her hat—*
       he sits near.

        You saved my life,—a debt
I am well content to owe.
 N.   Not so, my lord ;
I shared with my dear mother and my woman,
And your own servant, duties well repaid
In this your restoration.
 Lyn.   Yet methinks
I am not wholly cured.
 N.   What ails your lordship?
Doth your head ache?
 Lyn.   Not so. I merely crave
A draught of that ethereal soothing medicine
Made by a subtle mixture of fine sounds,
Which, gently poured into one's ears, doth rock
The brain to blissful dreaming and our soul
Breathes Paradise. Will you not sing one song?
This gentle servant, see, your lute, is ready—
     [*Takes down a lute from the wainscot*
      and touches the strings.
Or nearly. May I venture? (*Tunes it.*) Is that
 right?   [*Offers it.*
 N. My skill is somewhat homely as you know ;
Here's an old simple thing :
     [*She preludes a little, then sings.*

SONG.

I.

Wilt thou, Summer, haste away?
Yet a little longer stay.
Thou but camest yesterday—
    'Tis too soon to go.
Just as we were truly friends,
All our fine communion ends;
Autumn will not make amends,—
    Ah, I fear me, no!

II.

Leave thy hand in ours awhile;
Then at last a merry smile,
Parting sorrow to beguile,—
    Since it must be so.
We will hive thee in our heart,
Where is memory's better part,
Warm and loving as thou art,
    Through the winter snow.

Lyn. "O it came o'er my ear like the sweet South!"
—you know the line, I see. And your father is familiar as any cavalier with our fine stage-poet, who outsoars all best others as king eagle the whole tribe of hawks. He should be cavalier!

N. My father? That follows not. He is no precisian, but in principle firmer than oak.

Lyn. Would he were loyal!

N. So he is—to England. Would Charles Stuart were so!

Lyn. Could England do without her king?

N. Better than without truth and freedom!

Song.

AIR: *Mad Robin.* (The original words are lost.)

To be accompanied, if possible, by the singer on an old English lute; else (she fingering the lute) by a single harp in the orchestra.

1. Wilt thou, summer, haste a - way? Yet a lit-tle long-er stay;
2. Leave thy hand in ours a - while; Then at last a mer - ry smile,

Thou but camest yes-ter-day,— 'Tis too soon to go.
Part-ing sor-row to be-guile,—Since it must be so.

Just as we were tru - ly friends, All our fine com-munion ends;
We will hive thee in our heart, Where is mem'ry's bet-ter part,

Au-tumn will not make a-mends,—Ah, I fear me, no!
Warm and lov-ing as thou art, Through the win-ter snow.

Lyn. She hath had kings ever since the days of savagery, and grown great under them.

N. And changed them when needful. The country, my lord, exists not for the king's sake, but the king for the country's.

Lyn. A flag of truce, dear lady!

N. You count a woman not worth argument, my lord.

Lyn. I am humbler minded, believe me; I fear losing all my former convictions, ere I am aware. I talked mainly to support my own courage.

N. My father and you had much discourse when he was last here.

Lyn. I long for more of it. Comes he not home again soon?

N. Very soon—perhaps to-night. And to stay—to stay! unless some pressing call should summon him again, which heaven forefend! He hath fought in every battle from Edgehill, been thrice wounded; and now, needing rest and some care of his own affairs— the public stress being slackened—he hath been most honourably relieved of his charge.

Lyn. He is a brave soldier.

N. A brave man—not a *soldier!*

Lyn. How mean you, I pray?

N. He hath fought bravely in what he counts a great and just cause. So, my lord, have you. Mere *Soldiers* are the kind of men, made wolves or demons, that Tilly stormed Magdeburg with. Had not your Prince Rupert some like them? Let them go back to Germany or France and serve despotic kings—we like them not.

Lyn. (*Avoiding the subject.*) Nor I indeed. This is your father's likeness.

           [*Points to picture on wall: they rise*
                    and look at it.

N. In his handsome youth: but I like him still better now.

Lyn. Years have enriched his manly looks. He is
a wise and good man.

N. Indeed he is. Do you dispute much?

Lyn. At first I dared. But, tho' 'tis not easy to put
off the opinions one was born into, I soon saw how,
beyond reckoning, he encompassed me in experience,
overtopt me in knowledge, outweighed me in wisdom;
being most modest withal, and ever making too much
of my argument.

Enter GROME, *silently and unobserved.* [*He pretends to
be looking for something, but is really spying and
listening. He is in a plain dress, like a serving-man,
with a trace of the soldier.*]

N. Is't not pity, my lord, such men as you and he
    should stand at feud?—
Alas, what England hath already lost!

Lyn. I'm nothing: but indeed what gaps are made
By wild and wasteful war! had Falkland fall'n
By Frenchman's hand, how England would have wept
Had Spanish bullet struck John Hampden's breast,
How England like one man had mourn'd for him!
But now, half England—poor divided land,
A land beside itself—with frenzied shout
Joys when a noble Englishman is slain.

N. True, true! and who to blame?

Lyn.   Ambitious rebels!

N. No! an ambitious king—who would be more
Than England will endure in any king!

Lyn. (*Shaking his head.*) The time's perplext. But
    who is here, I pray you?
                [*Pointing to another picture.*

N. My uncle, Edward Clinton,—on the king's side;
Yet, strange to say! an honest man, I think.

Lyn. I well believe it. I have heard of him,
But never seen him.

N.   He's at Oxford now.

He sometimes writes a letter to my father,
Hoping to bend him to the royal side,—
Vainly enough. [*Sees* GROME *and addresses him.*
　　　　What seek you?
　Grome A key, madam, so please you. I think it is
not here.　　　　　　　　　　　　　　　 [*Exit.*
　Lyn. (*Gently.*) One other song?
　N.　　　　　　　　　　No more.
　Lyn. In sign of peace between us.
　N.　　　　　　　　Peace may there be!
Would it could overflow the land, like moonlight.
But no more songs to-night.　And further know
You must not tarry nigh an open window
When evening air grows moist.
　Lyn.　　　　　　　Why, I am well.
I'm almost sorry for it.
　N.　　　　　　　But not strong, sir.
I pray you now, come in; or must I call
Higher Authority?
　Lyn.　　　I yield to yours,
Madam, most willingly.
　　　　　　[*Both going towards side door* (L).
　　　　　　　Would I could think
I had a little of your father's favour.
　N. You have, sir.
　Lyn.　　　Do you think so?
　N.　　　　　I am sure of it.
He is your friend.—How autumn daylight dwindles!
Already half way to midwinter nights!
　Lyn. But every season hath its own delights.
　　　　　　　　[*Exeunt together.*
　　Same place.

Enter Colonel RADCLYFFE *in riding dress, looking joyful
and expectant. He exclaims "Home! home!" puts
down his gloves and hat, and calls in a louder voice—*

　　　　　　Lucy!

Enter Mistress RADCLYFFE *quickly. They embrace.*

My Lucy!

Mistr. R. This is like old days, my Basil!
A rough time hoards up sweets, like mountain honey
You're well?

Col. R. And happy!—Little do they know
Who deem that love is youth's particular;
The best of us must live to find what life is,
And then live on, to find what's best in life.

Mistr. R. Methinks you talk pure Devonshire to-
night.

Col. R. I am a poor Northampton man, no better.

Mistr. R. But thus you used to talk in Devonshire
How long is that ago?

Col. R.   A month or two—
A year or two—or is it twenty years?
They sometimes tell us life's a dream; but *love*—
We love each other, do we not? That's real!

Mistr. R. Thank God for it, sweet husband!
          Naseby Fight
Is like a dream now, though but three months past.
So will this war be, one day. How goes it on?

Col. R. Badly for Charles—who moves with stately
          step
And grave blind eyes, to ruin,—wiled along
By her, the black-eyed little Frenchwoman,
Their battle cry at Naseby. Could he put
Tom Wentworth's, my old schoolmate's, head again
Upon his shoulders and make use of him
To better purpose, Charles might have a chance!
'Tis idly said that on the eve of Naseby
Charles from his restless couch look'd up and saw
The ghost of him that served him—whom he mur-
          der'd—
Sadly and sternly gazing in his face.

Mistr. R. I do believe it.   Now and evermore
Pale Strafford haunts his dreams!
    Col. R.   *He* would have proved
A dangerous weapon in a skilful hand;
But Charles could only cut himself withal,
Then fling it down and break it!
> [*While saying this, he lifts his sword
> in the scabbard with his left hand,
> a short way, and lets it drop again
> to the hilt.*

    Mistr. R. You need not this!
> [*She unbuckles the sword and lays it
> on a chair.*

    Col. R. Nay not to-night, I hope!—But, our young
prisoner,—
What of *him*, Lucy?—Stay a little here.
    Mistr. R. Most gladly: but I'll shut the casements
    first.   [*Shuts them.*
    Col. R. Sound man again, I hear, thanks to your
    nursing.
    Mistr. R. His wound is heal'd, his dangerous fever
    cool'd.
Yes he is sound, I think, but scarcely strong.
    Col. R. 'Twill soon be boot and saddle, to horse and
    away.
Doth he not speak of that?
    Mistr. R.   Yes, much of late.
And whither goes he when exchanged?   To Rupert?
    Col. R. Bristol way, doubtless, to the horseman
    prince,
No wiser than his horse, who rides through foes
And leaves his friends to ruin, a campaign
Lost for a gallop.   Pity Lyndore must go!
The youth came out to please his elder brother,
Spurr'd headlong after Rupert, as a schoolboy
Follows the cock o' the school, caught up the phrases
Floating around him;—in the rights and wrongs,

All argument of quarrel, he was blank
As any clodpole forced to trail a pike.
—I say he *was* so : in this dangerous sickness
His mind hath measurably overshot
Its former stature.
   Mistr. R.   He hath conn'd that book
Of the king's letters.   Would he might go home
To Devon and be quiet!   He needs rest.
   Col. R. My Lord Lyndore, being what he is, must
    needs
Procure exchange (I marvel 'tis delayed),
Fill up his brother's place in Rupert's regiment,
Command the troop, men from his own estate,
Raised by his brother ; and in short must stand
Well forward in the party of the Court.
   Mistr. R. Poor boy !
   Col. R. How think you ?   Is his health restored ?
   Mistr. R. Safe from relapse, please Heaven, but far
    from strong.
   Col. R. You tended him right well.
   Mistr. R.   With cordial pleasure ;
And truly all of us have learnt to love him.
   Col. R. (*Pointedly.*) Doth Naomi love him ?
   Mistr. R.   Why ask that so sharply ?
   Col. R. Come, answer, wife.
   Mistr. R.   Basil, in sooth, I know not.
She hath not spoken word of it to me.
   Col. R. And yet it may be so.   I hope it is not !
                         [*They rise.*
   Mistr. R. Dear husband, look not anxious.   Have I
    done wrong ?
   Col. R. She is my dearest thing on earth, but one ;
Yet would I not withhold her from a suitor
Carrying Heaven's warrant clear to win and wear her.
A daughter's love we only hold in trust
Till it be claimed.   Alas ! it sometimes goes
Into a squanderer's hand.

Mistr. R.   You do not think
He's a court gallant, who would win and wear
A lady's favour like a knot of ribbon
Until the fashion pass'd ?   He is not such !
    Col. R. A brave youth ! and an honest one.
Mistr. R.   He is !
Be sure of it, dear husband !—Basil, think
How well I knew his mother, in whose kind blood
Was no sour drop !   [*He crosses.*
    Col. R.   I doubt it not, my Lucy.
But warily and wisely must we walk.
This youth's deservings are our very dangers.
Warn Naomi, I charge thee, Lucy, warn her
She look on Lord Lyndore as one whose course
Is mark'd by Providence to lead him off
From hers at the next turning ; nor build aught
Upon the sand-drift island of his visit.
Being gone, he'll soon take back his former self
(Or so much of it as concerns with action),
Range under Rupert's banner with flush'd cheek
His troop of tenants, cheering their new lord,
And—do as others do. Nay, circumstance
Is odds for most of us.—But where is *she ?*
Where's Naomi, " My Pleasantness ?"
    Mistr. R.   Return'd
From walking with Lyndore, and resting now.
                                    [*She sits.*
I accept thy reasons, Basil, yet I'm sure
There's more than this. Then why not tell me
    more ?
    Col. R. I have enemies—among the Parliament.
Mistr. R. Thou enemies !
    Col. R.   Ay, better men have had them.
I hear a blight hath crept upon my name ;
Hints of unsoundness, nay malignancy,
Which the diseased temper of the time
Makes partly credible.

Mistr. R. Who credits it?
Such falsehoods cannot hurt thee.
Col. R. I trust not.
But no man's safe.
[*He comes close and leans on her chair.*
And, mark this—of Lyndore too
Snake-whispers creep about men's itching ears.
Mistr. R. How framed?
Col. R. Diversely, as by forkèd tongue;
That he and I are plotting for the king.
Again, that I have drawn him *from* the king.
Mistr. R. You have been here but twice since he
took ill.
Col. R. (*With slow emphasis.*) That he hath lingered
in this house, avoiding
Loyal return to duty. And, moreover,
Our daughter's name, my Lucy, hath been used
To paint these falsehoods—he, she, you, and I,
Mixt in the scandal.
Mistr. R. (*Rising.*) Wholly false!
Col. R. Most false.
Yet now thou seest, my wife, how right it is
On all sides that if Lord Lyndore can move
He part as soon as possible.
Mistr. R. I fear so!
Col. R. Find Naomi, and speak to her at once.
Tell her Lyndore is leaving Ashby Manor.
Mistr. R. When, husband?
Col. R. Say to-morrow. Go, sweet wife,
I'll tarry here a little by myself. [*Kisses her.*
Good-bye, and not farewell—a short good-bye!
Mistr. R. (*Going: aside.*) Heav'n grant our daughter
had such good in store
As to her mother fell!—I'd ask no more. [*Exit.*
Col. R. (*Observes* GROME *in a corner of the room, who
has come in silently during the latter part of the dia-
logue.*) Who's there?

Grome. (*Coming forward a little.*) Shall I take off
your honour's boots?

Col. R. Nay, let be for the present. Thanks, my
man. Put this into my room.

> [*Gives his sword to* GROME, *who takes it
> most respectfully, and exit.*

Col. R. (*alone, pacing up and down*). Pray Heav'n she
　　　love him not!—it were a tangle
Hard to untie, and sharp to cut asunder.
I hold him dear, but dearer far my daughter;
And his good name, and ours, are *both* impeach'd
More deeply every day he stops with us.
We net the rich young lord! *He* shirks his duty,
Lull'd in the Puritan Armida's bower!—
Forge a malicious lie—ten thousand fools
Will back it instantly, agog to show
The vile sham-shrewdness of believing ill;
And in these times a lesser lie than this,
Like the small arrow puft through an Indian's tube,
May carry deadly venom.

> —Lord Lyndore!

> *Enter Lord* LYNDORE, *who runs to him and
> greets him warmly.*

Lyn. Dear Colonel Radclyffe!—let *me* play the
　　　host
For once, and welcome you to your own house!
No wonder if I almost think it mine.

Col. R. Who in broad England could have better right?
You're looking flesh and blood again, thank God.

Lyn. —And the most kind entreatment. I am well,
And must not longer be a burthen to you.

Col. R. Your lordship's still my prisoner; I remain
Your surety with the Parliament.

Lyn. 　　　　　　　　In faith
'Tis no uneasy prison—but were't other,
I would not break parole.

Col. R.   I fear it not.
But have you any news?
  Lyn.   Why, very little;
And that surprises me; for I have writ
To my cousin and to others, several times.
Thus much I know—Prince Rupert is at Bristol.
  Col. R. Is it your lordship's wish to join him there?
  Lyn. (*Somewhat surprised.*) Surely: when I have
once procured exchange.
  Col. R. I wrote to you from York, of that was
    proffer'd.
  Lyn. Proffer'd!—What proffer, pray you?
  Col. R.   'Twas proposed.
To exchange our Colonel Hodson, held by Rupert,
Against your lordship, when your health allow'd.
  Lyn. I never saw your letter!—when was't sent?
  Col. R. A fortnight since. I look'd for your reply—
But sickness was excuse enough.
  Lyn.   Excuse!
I have had no such letter—nor my cousin
Hath told me anything! I have written thrice
To London to him, *urging* an exchange.
You know Sir Geoffrey Percival—on your side,
And in the House?
  Col. R.   All this is very strange!
I'm glad I've come to-night. To own the truth,
My lord, the pressure of these times is such,
'Twere well, perhaps, no longer you delay
Your needful journey (would there were no need!)
—That is, suppose your strength allow it, fully.
  Lyn. I'd start to-night if I were free to go?
But how now, Colonel Radclyffe,—what's befallen?
  Col. R. O never doubt, Lyndore, our love for you!
Would that the world were made so, all could live
(As in a better world we hope to do)
Unsever'd, who are friends; since, to be friends—
What other reason makes true company?

                                      10—2

Good friends we are, good friends we shall remain,
I trust so ever—ever—(*takes his hand*)
                    Yet we must part,
And briefly—'tis your interest, do not doubt me.
   Lyn. I trust you, and obey you. But tell me more.
Am I suspected of—
   Col. R.   I'll tell you all
Presently, all I know. Meanwhile, this paper
                       [*Takes out paper.*
Signed by the General in command, will act
As your releasement, leaving the exchange
To Rupert, of some prisoner held by him
Of answerable rank. It came last night
                       [*Touches the paper.*
On my responsibility. And with it
              [*Separates second paper from first.*
A pass—yourself and servant—through our posts
Along the road to Bristol.
   Lyn.   I will start
To-morrow at day-break.
   Col. R.   This grieves me much.
In truth it does. We shall meet at supper time,
Or a little sooner.   [*Exit.*
   Lyn. (*Agitated.*) Now may the Devil—!
        [*Sees* GROME, *who has come in unobserved,*
         and is silently busying himself in an ob-
         scure part of the room.
What seek you, fellow?
   Grome. Only these, my lord—I ask your lordship's
pardon.   [*Takes up Colonel's hat and gloves*
               from chair and exit.
   Lyn. (*Alone.*)   What!
An exchange proffer'd and I not know of it.
Here lingering, tended like an ailing woman,
While Rupert and my regiment and my troop
At Bristol stand at bay! Have I been sleeping,
So that being call'd to, loudly, I heard nothing?

Nay, I am ready to go,—and have been ready
Any day since I tried to lift my arm,—
That's scarce a fortnight since ! Doth Radclyffe doubt
    me ?
He's far too noble ; but he knows past doubt
That others doubt me. Would I could start to-night !
(*Slowly*)—That means—take leave of Naomi—for
    ever.
We two are in two ships that glide away
On opposite courses. What a thing is life !
Radclyffe had argued with me many a time,
And more convinced me than he knows; yet now
Urges me back into the deadly ranks
Of his sworn enemies. And Naomi . . .
Suppose, as others of my class have done,
I changed sides, stept from one ship to the other,
Ere driven apart ?—Ay ! "left the sinking ship
As rats will !—saved his skin, and his estate.
The Parliament being master,—won besides
A Beauty with an orange breast-knot"—

                      Win her ?
She would despise me first and most of all !
O curse of public life, to make men slaves
Of their own repute, bid them distort themselves
To match some picture hung in others' brains !
Poor men are freer : who in all his realm
So hampered as the King ? I would to Heav'n
I were a neatherd on my own estate
And she a milkmaid ! O base thoughts ! how ill
Becoming her deserver. I believe
The worst they say of me perhaps is true,
And thus an honest conscience, turning lawyer,
Argues itself into a rogue ? Dear lady !

             Enter NAOMI.

N. My lord, I hear you leave us suddenly.

Lyn. It is so, madam ; hath your father told you ?
Early to-morrow,—with the break of dawn.

N. We shall be sorry to lose your company.

Lyn. I shall miss yours a thousand times a day !

N. Nay, 'twas an hour certain to come at last ;
Better without long warning. On your own part,
We'll wish you joy.

Lyn. How joy ?

N. In health restored,
Your place in life resumed,—tho' in some things
We would 'twere otherwise.

Lyn. (*Eagerly.*) How otherwise ?
What would you have me do ? Speak, I beseech you !

N. 'Tis not my part to give your lordship counsel.

Lyn. I would it were ; but tell me what you think
I pray you let me know your very thoughts.

N. They are worth little, when I know so little.
Hath not exchange been offer'd for your release ?

Lyn. Your father tells me,—I knew it not before.

N. And he hath got releasement in advance
And safeguard for your lordship, to rejoin
Your regiment at Bristol ?

Lyn. So it is.
You know, I think, a troop in it was raised
By my dead brother,—all of Devon men,
From his own hills, who freely follow'd him,
Giving their simple lives into his hand
To use them as he pleased. They fought right well,
Yeoman, and yeoman's son, and peasant lad ;
But Naseby Fight made havoc in their ranks,
And slew their captain. Still, they hold together,
" Lyndore's Troop,"—and the captainship is mine.
They wait for *me*. Shall I not go to them ?

N. How else ?

Lyn. How else indeed ? You see the case
Admits not of a day's, an hour's, delay ;
I ought to start to-night, I think !

N. (*With forced calmness.*)   My lord,
We see that you must needs pursue your path
We cannot wish the cause you fight for, well;
But, so far as the two may be disjoin'd,
We wish *you* well, my lord, unfeignedly.
—To-morrow, did you say?
   Lyn.   At earliest daylight.
   N. The time is short enough, and much to fill it.
So, my lord, for the present I shall leave you.
We'll give you kind farewells before you go.   [*Exit.*
   Lyn. Cold, cold, ice-cold! How could I take as real
The puppets of my fancy's theatre,
Myself had drest and spoke for, to amuse
The hours of slow recovery! Many scenes
Of love they play'd, all closed in happiness.
The true scene ends but poorly. Not one spark
Of love. Humanity!—yes, womankind
Is tender-hearted, dutiful, and sweet,—
She would have nursed a hospital as kindly;
Fool to imagine other! and now I see
Contempt fast growing as compassion fades,
To watch me idling here. (*Pause.*)—An odious war!
But I must ride to Rupert, fight my best,
And then—some whistling bullet or swift edge
Cut bonds, and free my soul! I thought she loved me
Fool!—fool!

Enter Naomi, *somewhat hastily.*

   N. Pardon, my lord—but one thing more
I meant to say, lest hurry leave it out—
Forget not that your sickness hath been grievous,
And new-grown health is but a tender plant.
So you will guard it prudently? If we
Took trouble for your health, methinks we hold
Some property therein.
   Lyn. And will you care
For news of me?

N. Indeed, we'll look for it
From day to day—all of us in this house—
Most earnestly.   *[Going.*

    Lyn. (*Following a step or two.*) O Naomi! one word.
Now—now—before we part. It is perhaps
The very last time we're alone together;
You'll listen to me? Yes?—

                *[Takes her hand in both of his : she
                   turns her head away and looks
                   sorrowful and frightened.*

N. No, no, my lord !
    Lyn. I tremble to offend you, yet I'll speak—
You know—you *must* know that I   . . .

    Enter Colonel RADCLYFFE *in an in-door dress.*

    Col. R. (*In a mild firm voice.*) Naomi !
Thy mother asks for thee ; she's in her chamber.
                [Exit NAOMI, *curtsying to Lord* LYNDORE,
                   who bows profoundly.*
Pardon, my lord ; I'm loth to be so rude,
But 'tis no common case. (*Approaches him.*) Dear
    Lord Lyndore !
I'll use a freedom with you I would shun
With one less loved ; for boldly let me say
I love you—every parting hath some tinge
Of death's own frankness in it, the great parting—
So doth my wife. And further still I'll push
The time's allowance and confess to you
My daughter is most friendly in her thoughts.
—But, in addition, I must tell you this,—
There can be nothing of a closer bond
Between you.
    Lyn.   Oh, sir, she's dearer than my life !
    Col. R. You have not told her this?
    Lyn.   I have not dared.
    Col. R. Then, I entreat you, never tell her so.

Ask not for reasons; which, at least in part,
Your mind will prompt you in ; but hold this sure—
That such a marriage must not, cannot be.

Lyn. Cannot!—O let me see her—from her mouth
Receive my sentence. Grant me this at least.

Col. R. It must not be. In brief, my lord, unless
You bid my daughter farewell in the key
Of quiet friendship, no half-tone beyond,—
I'll carry your adieu. You shall not see her.

Lyn. Not see her!—not see Naomi again ! . . .
Doth Mistress Radclyffe know of this ?

Col. R. She doth.
I speak for her as for myself.

Lyn. Good God !
How little knew I how confused our path is !
I thought one merely had to step straight on
And take his fortune ! Radclyffe, am I a coward ?

Col. R. Let no man say so in my hearing,—else
He shall abye it.

Lyn. No ! I am not that—
Unless my nerves are weaken'd. Formerly
When swords were out and horses on the fret,
Our trumpet thrill'd no nerve save to ride in
Upon the gleaming pikes and levell'd guns,
Where twenty thousand men were brave as I !

Col. R. Needless to tell me : if my life again
Hung on your courage, I should fear no scaith.

Lyn. (*Excitedly.*) But others deem not so. I pass
    for one
Who slinks aside and leaves his men in danger.
My name is doubtless in the garrison
Hung round with sneers, a tatter'd effigy
The common soldiers hoot and spit upon ;
And those of my own rank would scorch me up
With one contemptuous look if I came near (*pause*).
(*Suddenly in another tone.*)—Why should I go to them !

Col. R. Because you must.

Lyn. You tell me so.

Col. R.   Could I at such a point
In your affairs persuade you *not* to go ?

Lyn. Nay, but suppose, Radclyffe,—I say suppose—
A man in my place, who should find his aims,
His hopes, his purposes, his inmost thoughts,
Alter'd—

    Col. R. (Perplexed and vexed.) Nay—do not tell me
      this, Lyndore !   [*Crosses.*

    Lyn. (With rapid and impassioned utterance.)
To whom else could I tell it ?   Are you not
The first man who awaken'd in my soul
(Even more by what you are than what you said)
The faculty of reason ?—some true glimpse
Of what life is and ought to be, some sense
Of what we owe to others, and to Heav'n,
Some light to help me onward through the maze
And mist ?—I must speak out !—
(More quietly.)   When I came here
Three months ago, you know not what I was,—
A foolish, flashy thing, lighter than froth !
The manners of this house, grave, pure, and sweet,
The creatures it enshrines, who would be saints
Were they less kindly human,—that keen look
At all things from death's door, wherein they take
A strange new perspective,—the tranquil days
Of slow recovery, second infancy
With a man's brain and heart to breathe its air,—
O Radclyffe !   I am changed, another man.
And why—

    Col. R. (Much disturbed.)   No more, no more !

Lyn.   O speak !

Col. R.   How speak ?
Would thou hadst left me to my fate !—
                No, no,
Forgive, I talk at random !—but indeed
I am perplex'd beyond all use of words.

Lyn. Your counsel, sir, shall be my oracle.

Col. R. (*Vehemently*). It shall not!—
    (*Then more mildly, collecting himself,*
    but with earnest expression)
    See, Lyndore,—this is no case
Where friend asks friend's advice, and there an end.
Consider what you are, and what I am,
(Plain words are best) with all eyes fix'd upon us,
Slander already busy. All at once,
You change sides—underneath my roof!—what then?

Lyn. (*Abandoning himself for the moment to despondency.*)
      I know not!—care not!

Col. R. (*Collecting himself entirely, and with great gravity and dignity.*) Well then, Lord Lyndore—
Since I must speak for you—I am resolved.

Lyn. (*Eagerly expecting his further words.*)
      And I'll obey!

Col. R.   Then give me your free pass—
And the release—   [*He does so.*
    They're henceforth null and void.
    [*Puts them into his breast pocket.*

Lyn. But, sir!—

Col. R.   I'll take upon me to make out
Another pass—for York, not Bristol.

Lyn.   York?

Col. R. Our General's head-quarters; he will take
Charge of your lordship henceforth; and 'twere best
You start to-night. I'll write your papers now.
      [*Sits down to table.*

Lyn. (*Aside.*) He scorns me!—I deserve it!
    (*Aloud*) Colonel Radclyffe,
I thank you deeply; and I will be ready
At eight o'clock to-night.

Col. R.   For York?

Lyn.   For Bristol.

Col. R. (*Standing up.*) Here are your papers.
    [*Giving back the papers he had taken.*

Lyn. (*Looking round.*) I must find some one to —
Ah !

> [*Sees* GROME *again in the room,
> pretending to hang up a whip or
> something on the wall ;* GROME
> *turns and bows ;* Lord LYNDORE
> *addresses him.*

Where is my man ?

Grome. Gone out, my lord, I believe.

Lyn. When he returns, send him to me at once.

Grome. Yes, my lord.   [*Exit, bowing humbly.*

Enter Mistress RADCLYFFE *and* NAOMI.

Mistr. R. (*Taking Lord* LYNDORE'*s hand in both of
hers.*)   To-morrow morning !
It is very soon.

Lyn. Madam, I go *to-night.*

N. (*With sudden emotion.*)   To-night !

Mistr. R.   To-night !

Col. R. (*Interposing.*) There are good reasons for it.
(*To Lord* LYNDORE.)   May I request your ear, my lord,
   one instant ?   [*They go up.*

N. You see he hurries off.

Mistr. R.   Against his will.

N. (*Somewhat bewildered.*) It may be so :—and you
   are sorry for it—
Are you not. mother ?

Mistr. R. (*With great feeling.*) If my own dear boy
Were living, and grown up, and parting thus,
'Twere scarce more bitter !

N. Can it be to-night ?

Mistr. R. Hush, darling !

> [*Goes a step or two towards the men, who
> are still in grave, slow conversation in
> the background.*

We came to bid you to supper.

Col. R. (Coming forward with Lord LYNDORE.)
Thanks, my Lucy.

Mistr. R. (Looks affectionately at Lord LYNDORE.)
My lord, may I have your company?

Lyn. (Smiling sadly.) For the last time!

[*They move to door.*

Col. R. (Tenderly to NAOMI.) Come, daughter.
(*Going, they pause.*) You trust me, dear—even if I
make you unhappy.

N. I trust you entirely! [*They follow.*

[*Exeunt Mistress* RADCLYFFE *with Lord* LYNDORE,
followed by Colonel RADCLYFFE *and* NAOMI.
As they go, GROME *appears, standing half con-
cealed behind a tall chair, and looks after them
knavishly, whilst scene-drop slowly descends.*

END OF SCENE I.

SCENE II.

[*A fine old panelled room or gallery in the Manor House, with
pictures, and armour and some rows of large books. Practicable
doors* R *and* L. *A recess near centre of back, with a window in
it, and two large old pictures. A trophy of swords on the wall,
in the recess or close to it. Old furniture—but not too much of it.*

PRUDENCE *discovered, finishing some settling
of things.*

P. This room wunt be left to issel so much, now
master's come home.

Enter TOM, *hat in hand, as if just come into
house.*

Tom. Zo, Prue! I've a just got back. We can 'a
two minutes' quiet chat, can't us? We're old friends
like, now, Prue, bean't us? Zimmeth a couple o' years,
'fegs, zince master and me took shelter here.

P. Ah dear, dear, what a day wur that! I wur
raight frightened o' thee at first, measter Trivet.

Tom. Vrighted, Prue?

P. Ah—thinks I, here's some o' the hell-babes under
our roof at last!—the swagg'rin', swearin', drinkin',
gamblin', roysterin'—

Tom. (*Shakes his head.*) No, no, not me!

P. Ah, some of ye.

Tom. Not me. But I were vrighted too, at thoughts
o' biding here. Long prayers and short commons,
thinks I. But the smell o' dinner encouraged me
like; and when I tastis your home-brew, "They're
vellow-creatures!" I zays—and zo I've vound ye, Prue,
I will zay.

P. O, measter's none of your hard ones.—Your
young gentleman's as good as well now; fever clean
gone; hands as cool, and pulse as quiet as mine.

Tom. Let's veel thy pulse.

P. That ain't to the purpose. He'll be for moving
shortly. Where to?

Tom. To Devonsheer, if I'd my wa-y. But, lookeezee,
Prue, we be what they calls Pris'ners o' War. I'll explain theeze matter to 'ee. (*Comes close.*) You have
us and hold us, you zee (*takes her hand*), and wunt free
us on no account whatsumdever—(*She nods several
times.*)—'Cause we be on wrong zide—that's to zay,
raight zide,—I means, *t'other* zide. You keeps hold
on us, taight, taight as you plaise; but still, you does
us no harm; you don't hurt us—nornabit? (*Still
holding her hand.*)

P. Oh—I used to think prisoners were allays shot
or hanged, or their heads cut off, poor things!

Tom. Not 'mong Chrissen volk—'cept they 'appens

to be short in temper. You keeps us pris'ners and uses us well—Don't 'ee tek' awa-y thee hand—and we 'ul do zame by you (*pats her hand*), and zo theas meks war quite comfortable like, leastways to what it might be.

P. Ah, 'tis bad enough business, measter Trivet. I hopes we'll see no more on't. (*Takes her hand away.*) What sort o' place now is Devonshire?

Tom. A lovely zweet place, that's a zure thing! and no zweeter spot in't than our Park. I can zee't now, th' old red Hall at wood-edge, big rocky tors on moor above, and clear river galloping to the zay at valley's end. I've a work'd there man and boy, vather and gramfer avore me. But you'll want to know whereabout I do bide: I've a cottage and garden. That's not much, you'll zay; but I'm to have a pritty plat o' ground when we gets back—and do'ee know what I means to do?

P. How should I, measter Trivet?

Tom. Build an offshoot to my cottage. You'll ask me, what for? and I'll tell 'ee,—to get more room. Why more room? zays you,—an' I'll tell 'ee—I'm thinking of matteremōny.

P. Eh, measter Trivet, what's that?

Tom. Gett'n married, Prudence; nayther more nor less. (*Confidentially.*) Besides t' land, his lordship's as good as promised me gardener's place. I'se a pritty turn thic wa-y, if you'll believe me.

> [PRUDENCE *has been softening and inclining to him, but* GROME *enters behind during* TOM'S *last speech and watches them, seen by* PRUDENCE, *not by* TOM. *Her manner changes.*

P. (*Coldly.*) Oh, very likely.

Tom. Old gardener at Lyndore's a useless old chap.

P. So let un be. I care not!

Tom. Good now, Prue, what's wrong?

Grome. (*Comes forward, smiling civilly.*) I humbly ask your pardons both for interrupting: I came to look for Tom Trivet.

Tom. (*Roughly.*) Well, now you've vound him, Paul Grome, what d'ye want wi' him?

Grome. (*To* PRUDENCE.) My Rose of Sharon! (*whispers*) I have somewhat to say to thee.

P. I must go. Good be with you both!

[*Runs off.*

Grome. Good master Trivet, I would fain be thy good friend.

Tom. Thou'rt too good for me.

Grome. Alas, a worm, a worm!

Tom. Very like—but laive off squirming!—I bean't o' your wa-ys o' thinking and never sholl.

Grome. (*Unctuously.*) Alas, I know thy lot hath been cast in evil places, among the Canaanites and Hittites and Amorites—

Tom. No zuch thing!

Grome. The Peruzites and the Jebusites—

Tom. Devil a bit!

Grome. And the Hivites. But the Lord may yet be pleased to open thine eyes.

Tom. Lookeedeezee, Paul Grome, my eyes mayn't want opening zo much as you think vor. I can zee there's underhand business a-going on in theas old house.

Grome. Underhand business, master Trivet! Of what nature?

Tom. Ay, tell me that! One thing I do know— I often catch thee a-sliding and a-sneaking about like a tom-cat, creeping in at this corner, vanishing round t'other,—

Grome. (*Aside.*) Damn the booby! (*Aloud.*) You are merry this evening, master Trivet.

Tom. Not particklar, Paul Grome.—You've been a long while from your regiment, ha'n't you?

11

Grome. (*Hastily.*) What the—— ! (*Quietly.*) 'Tis in garrison ; and the honoured lady here, extending favour to the unworthy, hath wished my stay.

Tom. (*In undertone.*) Ay, women takes up curous notions. Thou'st wriggled into favour sure enough. (*Louder.*) Aisy times, Grome ; to Rugby or Leicester twice a week wi' letter-bag—don'no' what else thou doest, more'n lob about.

Grome (*Mutters.*) The scoundrel would pick a quarrel. (*Louder, suarely.*) Master Trivet, my lord desired to see thee the moment thou wast returned.

Tom. Ass ! couldn' ye a' zaid zo ?   [*Hurries off.*

Grome (*Speaking after him.*) You appeared to be engaged, master Trivet ! (*Alone.*) These fools give a deal of trouble. He must meddle with my young woman too. I'll stop that. Neither shall he miss his share of the rod in pickle.

> [*During the delivery of the following words,* GROME *shifts his position occasionally, without noise, listening at the doors, and prying into various parts of the room.*

What's Charlton going to do ? He must be quick about it. I gave him three days' notice of the Colonel's coming home. Here's another letter for him, though never meant for him—(*takes letter from pocket and looks at it*)—but how to let him have it ? He may be hovering about. Very likely. He's devilish fond of hovering about. (*Puts up letter.*) I'm shown little of his schemes, the patch of light round a miner at work,—but I hold my lamp up when his back's turned.

I'll wait here till they come from supper. (*Sits down.*) I have his little plan on my thumb-nail. Uncle and rival clapt in the Tower (not through *him*, O no !) for this pretended plot against Parliament, there they lie safe enough, out of rogue Charlton's way. No

man living he fears like his uncle; but he cares no
longer for the girl, I can see that.

As the real plot ripens, a breath of air may puff
these two heads off, and make Charlton rid of two
plaguey fellow-creatures, Lord of Ashby Manor, and,
by-and-by, one of the grateful Royalty's new peers.
All plain sailing enough, if the weather serve. In any
case he stakes on the King, and I daresay he's right.
England will soon tire of psalm singing and go back to
her jolly old ways. (*Rises.*) What an honest fellow our
gallant captain is! And Grome his accomplice?—a
poor devil that pries, and filches, and makes his petty
profit. What knows he of those great affairs—save by
chance? The sun-royal will never shine on Grome,
save in the shape of a few jacobuses. Would 1 were
in Holland now, and these in my pocket.

[*It has been growing dusk since* GROME
*came in. Servants enter with tapers and
light the sconces.* GROME *pretends to be
arranging something and hangs about.
Exeunt servants.* GROME *continues:*

—One thing fairly puzzles me!—if this young fellow
rides off now, what becomes of our fine scheme?
Charlton, after all, may only show himself a clever
fool, like so many more of us! I sometimes almost
wish I was honest myself: only, it ties a man down
so confoundedly!

*Re-enter Servants and set other lights on table—Enter
Colonel* RADCLYFFE *and Lord* LYNDORE *in riding
dress, speaking.*

Col. R. —Believe it!

Lyn. I thank thee, Radclyffe, from my heart!

Col. R. Our love runs level, dear Lyndore. Enough
said. Each to his duty. I hear my wife and daughter
coming: take leave at once, and briefly.

Lyn. Partings may be for ever!—I'll obey you.

   Enter Mistress RADCLYFFE *and* NAOMI.

Col. R. Lucy, my Lord Lyndore will take leave of
you now. His man, he tells me, hath the horses ready,
or very nearly.

Lyn. All is prepared.

Col. R. The weather holds fair, and a moon rising.
He but rides to Daventry, where he will find good
quarters for the night.

Mistr. R. We part with you unwillingly, my dear
lord.

Lyn. I am heartily sorry to leave you, and most
grateful,—both beyond all words. Farewell, dear
madam! (*Kisses her hand.*) (*To* NAOMI.) Farewell.
           [*Kisses her hand.*

N. God keep you, sir.

Col. R. Short parting's best; so come with me,
Lyndore.

Lyn. (*Aside.*) I leave a house which I may see no
more.   [*They move towards door* (L).

N. How far is it to Bristol, mother?

Mistr. R. Two days' journey.

N. Who commands the besiegers?

Mistr. R.   Come, daughter.

N. Gone! [*Hides her face on her mother's neck.*
    [*Col.* RADCLYFFE *and Lord* LYNDORE
      approach door (L); *when near it,*
      door opens and servant appears,
      flurried.

Servant. So please your honours—
    [*A young Cavalry Officer of the Par-*
      liament has just dismounted, steps
      before him and interrupts. Soldiers
      are seen behind him. The ladies
      come forward anxiously.

Officer. (*A self-important person.*) Your pardon, ladies. Best speak for myself. I come here by authority.

Col. R. Who are you, sir?

Officer. Colonel Radclyffe, your servant—you will understand my duty. I am Joshua Brand-from-the-Burning Jebb, Cornet, in command of an escort of dragoons.

Col. R. Whom escort you, sir?

Cornet. Sir Thomas Chenery, Colonel Radclyffe, honourable commissioner for the Parliament; who hath especial business in this neighbourhood, and by whose orders we have made bold to visit your house.

Col. R. An unexpected honour; but you are welcome, sir.

Cornet. I must request that no one quit this room.

Lyn. How, sir?

Cornet. My Lord Lyndore, if I mistake not, (*Lord* LYNDORE *bows*) a prisoner of war. Under this warrant, my lord, (*shows it*) I am ordered to carry you to London with all possible despatch.

> [*Signs to soldiers, two of whom place themselves beside Lord* LYNDORE.

Lyn. To London! (*All exclaim.*)

Cornet. This, Colonel Radclyffe, is my authority for thus entering your house (*shows another paper*)—most unwillingly—and further . . .

Col. R. Go on, sir.

Cornet. For arresting you.

> [*Signs to soldiers; two of whom now place themselves beside the Colonel.*

Col. R. Arresting me! on what charge?

Cornet. Colonel Radclyffe, hold me excused for the present, I pray you.

Mistr. R. Basil!

Col. R. Fear nothing, Lucy. (*To his daughter.*) Good cheer, my Naomi!

N. They will not carry you away?—They cannot harm him, mother?

Mistr. R. Alas, many innocent men lie in prison on mere suspicion.

Lyn. (*To Colonel* RADCLYFFE.) You comprehend this, Radclyffe?

Col. R. The least part of it. I told you there were evil tongues at work.

Lyn. Have I brought this upon you?

> [CORNET, *at back of stage, has meanwhile been quietly sending off soldiers to various parts of the house, posts two at each door of the room, and keeps three with him.*

Cornet. (*Comes down, and interposes between* LYNDORE *and* RADCLYFFE.) Hold me excused, gentlemen! (*To* LYNDORE.) 'Twould seem your lordship is prepared for a journey.

Lyn. I was at point to start, sir.

Cornet. In-deed! Might I venture to inquire—whither?

Col. R. With your favour, sir, *I* can briefly explain this. Lord Lyndore was setting forth towards Bristol with a release and pass signed by the General,—exchange to be completed on his arrival. They were given on my responsibility.

Cornet. In-deed!

Col. R. What mean you, sir?

Cornet. Hold me excused, Colonel. Those papers are useless now—altogether useless.

N. (*To her mother, meanwhile.*) He were better in London than Bristol?

Mistr. R. I know not, child. Ill-agents are at work. Think of thy father, Naomi.

N. I do, mother, I do.

Enter Tom (L.), *after a short parley with the sentries, in riding-dress, a valise in his hand.*

Tom. Zo plaise you, my lord,—

Cornet. Is this your lordship's man? With your leave— [*Tries to take valise.*

Tom. (*Swings it away.*) Let be! let be!—Tantara-bobus again!

Cornet. (*Motions to soldiers, who seize* Tom—*valise is taken.*) Hath your lordship papers here?

Lyn. Papers?—none of moment, certainly. Look for yourself, sir. [*Gives key.*

Cornet. (*Examining valise.*) A packet of letters—and, among them, a paper in cypher.

Lyn. (*Looking.*) I know it not.

Tom. Roguery, I'll swear!

Cornet. (*Still looking at cypher.*) Hm, hm, yes, yes—It so happens I have the key to *this.*

[*General movement.*

Col. R. and Lyn. What is it?

Cornet. Confirmation—full confirmation.

Lyn. Of what?

Cornet. Of a most grave charge. Lord Lyndore, Colonel Radclyffe, I must at once put you separately into close arrest. Look to them! [*To the soldiers.*

Col. R. What charge, sir?

Cornet. The man too.

[*Lord* Lyndore, *Colonel* Radclyffe, *and* Tom *are guarded separately.*

Tom. Odswilderakins! 'tis the wursest piece 'o' business yet!

Mistr. R. My head swims.

[*Sinks into a chair.*

Col. R. (*Soothingly*). Lucy!

N. (*Approaching Cornet.*) Are you advised in what you do, sir? What are these gentlemen charged with?

Cornet. Your name, fair mistress, an't please you?

N. I am Colonel Radclyffe's daughter

Cornet. (*Looking at her deliberately.*) Ah! *you* are Colonel Radclyffe's daughter.

N. (*Hotly.*) Ay, sir!—and if I were his son——

Mistr. R. Naomi, come to me, I pray thee.

N. (*Moving towards her mother.*) Is this fledgling officer to twirl Colonel Radclyffe and Lord Lyndore round his fingers without reason given?

Cornet. (*Touching the paper taken from valise.*) Here is reason enough—more than enough.

Lyn. I never saw that paper in my life before.

Col. R. (*To Cornet, with authority.*) Say in plain words, sir, what you mean.

Cornet. Colonel Radclyffe and my Lord Lyndore, you are charged with plotting against the Parliament and the peace of the kingdom. In this paper is full confirmation of the suspected plot—fullest confirmation.

Col. R. Plot?

Cornet.—For raising the Midland Counties against Parliament, seizing certain garrisons and strong places, and reinforcing the king at Oxford.

Mistr. R. Plot? And who joins that word with Colonel Radclyffe's name?

Cornet. It hath been so joined.

N. Only by fools or knaves!

Col. R. The charge is groundless. But what next, sir?

Cornet. I await the Honourable Commissioner. Meanwhile I must put the house under strict ward, and make bold to ask for all keys. Find me pen and paper. (*Soldier brings writing materials; Cornet writes at table.*) Remove the prisoners for the present and guard them in separate rooms.

[*Exeunt some soldiers with Col.* Radclyffe *and Lord* Lyndore. *Meanwhile* Naomi (R) *has given way and is weeping.*

Mistr. R. (*Consoling her.*) Hush, my child, the false

charges will easily be dispelled. As for Lord Lyndore,
it *is* better he should go to London than Bristol. He
is all unfit for war and hardship.

N. True, alas!—and yet he longs to go.

Mistr. R. He longs to be at Bristol with his men.

N. And rightly, rightly! so would I.—O mother
Can there be duty on the wrongful side?
Are this and that side, chances in a game?
Do we take sides by hazard?

Mistr. R.   Not so, daughter.
Conscience must rule; the rest is in God's hand.

N. It is, and must be. If he go to London
Is he in danger there?

Mistr. R.   In none, I think.

N. What will befall him?

Mistr. R.   Only questionings.
Delays and doubts, not hard to solve at last.
Daughter, I'm very glad he goes to London!
Herein I see the hand of Providence.
Send him to Bristol and they drive from port
A shatter'd vessel into raging storm.

N. Thank God he goes not thither!

Cornet. (*Pauses in writing, looks up and addresses
Mistress* RADCLYFFE.) Madam, with your favour.

> [*Mistress* RADCLYFFE *approaches him, leaving*
> NAOMI *near the front.*

How many servants in your house?

> [*He motions her to sit, she refuses: he then
> asks her questions and notes down her
> answers. Meanwhile—*

N. (*Soliloq.*) To Bristol?—or to London?—either
   way
And every way so far away from me!
And what am I to him? . . . O foolish girl!
Can this be Naomi Radclyffe? Where's my pride.
My old composure? Doth this feverous war
Lay hold upon my blood, make my heart throb,

And all swim round unsettled? What to seize
And steady me by grasping it I know not!
I know his wishes have no harbour here,
But shoot adown the wind to Bristol gates,
And overleap the leaguered city-wall
Compass'd with fiery death. My dream last night
Was dark and doleful; and when he is gone
I may not speak of him,—when he is dead
What right have I to weep for him? O Heaven,
Be merciful, and teach me what to do,
Or how to rest! In which room is he guarded?—
Would he were now upon the road to London,
Prisoner, but safe!—to Bristol is to death!

Mistr. R. (*Returning from back.*) Come now, my daughter.

[*Exeunt Mistress* RADCLYFFE *and* NAOMI.

Cornet. (*Finishing his writing and standing up.*) I'll have a word with Lord Lyndore. Call back his guard —(*to soldier, who goes out*). He may desire to communicate with me in private.

Re-enter Lord LYNDORE, *guarded.*

Cornet. (*To soldiers.*) Wait without. (*To Lord LYN-DORE, in undertone.*) Hath your lordship, peradventure, ought to say to me?

Lyn. Only, sir, that this paper you have found is absolutely strange to me; as is the pretended plot whereof it treats.

Cornet. (*Drily.*) Hold me excused, my lord! I merely wish to give you an opportunity, if there be anything to communicate.

Lyn. There is nothing, sir.

Cornet. Very well, my lord. Your escort will be ready as soon as our horses are fed—say in an hour's time. Meanwhile be good enough to rest here. This room shall be yours. I am going. Sentries, to your posts. Your servant.

Lyn. One word, sir,—as to Colonel Radclyffe—

Cornet. Hold me excused, I pray you!—Your servant.   [*Exit.*

Lyn. (*Alone: restless and agitated.*)

Ten minutes since it seemed a martyrdom
To quit this house perforce—as now to stay.
I reck not of this plot, if plot there be ;
Nor of the grim reality of the Tower,
Whose stony jaws shut fast on innocence
As well as guilt, and let no cry escape :
But not to be at Bristol with my men !
My honour there with Rupert stands at risk,
Myself being absent—" Safe enough " they'll say ;
" He's but one other noble renegade,
Since fortune left the king !"

> [*Pacing the room, during these words, he opens door* (L) *and finds a sentry ; shuts it, approaches opposite door, stops, makes a gesture with his hand implying that it is useless to attempt escape and sits down sadly. Door* (R) *opens, someone is seen parleying in dumb show with sentry, then* NAOMI *comes in hurriedly.* LYNDORE, *astonished, rises and makes a step or two to meet her ; the sentry follows* NAOMI *into the room and then stands stolidly, keeping his eye upon both.*

Lyn. Naomi !

N. (*Agitated, in undertone.*) I have but a moment. Are you—would you still go to Bristol?

Lyn. Sooner than to Heaven !

N. Ah !—In London—

Lyn. I shall be in prison, and all my slanderers at large.

N. Consider, Bristol is beleagured, and you—

Lyn. Have the more call to be there ! You do not recollect my urgency.

N. I do—most clearly. You have still your Pass?

Lyn. Safe—here.   [*Touches his breast.*
N. Hide this, and read it when I go.
                         [*Passes a note to him.*
Sentry. (*Advancing.*) Now, mistress.
N. Farewell!
Lyn. Farewell, dear lady!
          [*She goes, followed by sentry, they pass out
          and the door is closed. A mutual gesture
          of farewell before* NAOMI *disappears.*

Lyn. (*Reading note.*) "Right hand picture in the
recess—press the carved rose on its frame. Secret
stair—stable-yard—I have released your man, and he
and the horses are ready. The men below know not
as yet of your arrest. Your pass will serve you. Be
quick!"
A way of escape! At least a chance! (*Looks round.*)
With a free start 'twill be hard to overtake us. For
Bristol and my men!—
          [*Presses on carved rose; picture turns on ver-
          tical axis and shows a narrow stair descend-
          ing in the wall.* LYNDORE *turns towards
          door where* NAOMI *disappeared, and says
          with heartfelt expression, though in under-
          tone:*
Farewell, my own sweet NAOMI!
          [CHARLTON RADCLYFFE *mean while is seen by
          the audience in the recess behind the picture
          and on* LYNDORE *turning again to the open-
          ing he finds* CHARLTON *standing there, in
          riding-dress, sword in hand.*
Lyn. You here, sir?
          [*They speak in suppressed tones, but with
          gradually increasing anger.*
Ch. Yes, my lord, as it happens. I know the ways
of this house. But mistake me not. I would not stop
you. My uncle and you are arrested.—Go, my lord,
and leave him to his fate. I'll make way for you.

Lyn. The charge is false and foolish.

Ch. Very likely, my lord. Go—the stair is free—I'll say nothing.

Lyn. I will not go!

Ch. You lose time, my lord. The road is still clear.

Lyn. Enough, sir! trouble me no farther.

Ch. Do you distrust me?

Lyn. Profoundly!

Ch. (*As going.*) Farewell, my lord!—(*turns to Lord* LYNDORE *again.*) One word more—you have play'd a noble part here!

Lyn. What mean you, sir?

Ch. (*Losing temper.*) While miching, on pretence of illness, you have striven to beguile my cousin,—

Lyn. What, sir!

Ch.—You have hurt, perhaps fatally, my uncle's reputation;—thus outraging hospitality and trust and every principle of honour. And now you would have slunk off like a thief!

Lyn. You speak falsely and foully!

Ch. Bitter truths, my lord!

Lyn. Base lies!—for the which I hope one day to call you to account. Take this in pledge!

[*Flings a riding glove (they were stuck in his belt) in* CHARLTON'S *face.*

Ch. (*Leaps down from picture, which closes behind him, seizes Lord* LYNDORE *with left hand, and raises his sword menacingly.*) Scoundrel! if you had a sword!

Lyn. (*Flinging him off so that he staggers back, and snatching a sword from trophy.*) I have!

[*They fight: sentries rush in, and at the same moment Lord* LYNDORE *wounds* CHARLTON *in the right arm, who stumbles and falls, dropping his sword. Others enter by various doors, including* GROME, *who puts himself forward in assisting* CHARLTON.

Grome. (*Mutters.*) What the devil has he been doing? A plotter should keep his temper.

Enter Mistress RADCLYFFE *and* NAOMI, *and* PRUDENCE.

N. (*Rushing up to* LYNDORE.) Are you hurt?

Lyn. (*Smiling joyfully.*) Unhurt!

> [*As she leans forward to put the question he presses her for a moment to his breast.*

Mistr. R. Charlton here!—and wounded!

> [*She and* NAOMI *and* PRUDENCE *kneel to help* CHARLTON; *the Cornet also helps;* CHARLTON's *arm is bandaged with a scarf, and he is propt up.*

Movement at door (L), *soldiers make way and draw themselves up. Enter Sir* THOMAS CHENERY, *a dignified elderly man, and his Secretary, Mr.* JOHN CHAD, *a dry, keen-looking lawyer of about* 40, *who puts on spectacles occasionally but never changes feature.*

Cornet. (*Saluting.*) The Honourable Commissioner of the Parliament.

Sir Thomas Chenery. What's this?—resistance?— Your pardon, ladies. Why, how comes Captain Radclyffe here?

Cornet. I know not, Sir Thomas. I thought he was at Leicester. Look on this, sir, I pray you.

> [*Shows paper taken from valise to Sir* THOMAS, *who consults Secretary a moment.*

Sir Thomas. Where is Colonel Radclyffe?

Cornet. (*Motioning to soldiers, who open a little.*) There, Sir Thomas.

Col. R. (*They speak as old acquaintances.*) Your servant, Sir Thomas.

Sir Thomas. Yours, Colonel Radclyffe.

Col. R. My Lord Lyndore. [*Presenting him.*

Sir Thomas. Your servant, my lord. Colonel Radclyffe, I never before was unwilling to look upon your face. This is my secretary, Mr. Chad, learned in the law. Your name, Colonel Radclyffe, is given in, with my Lord Lyndore's, among the chief ones in this plot against the Parliament.

Col. R. As to the plot, Sir Thomas, I have heard of none such before this evening, and I own scarce believe in it.

Sir Thomas. A plot is certain.

Secretary. Ab-so-lute-ly.

Sir Thomas. If you can free yourself, no one will rejoice more than I. I fear I cannot choose but send you and his lordship to London. But can you explain this? [*Points to* CHARLTON, *who is still on the ground.*

Col. R. Pure enigma to me.

Cornet. (*By* CHARLTON.) 'Tis but a flesh wound, Sir Thomas. The Captain struck his head in falling and was stunned, but he recovers.

[*They lift* CHARLTON *to a chair—while tending him and adjusting his dress a letter falls out,* GROME *picks it up and conceals it.*

N. (*Steps forward.*) What hast thou there, fellow?

Grome. Nothing, madam.

N. A letter.

Grome. No, madam.

N. Thou hast. Give it up! Here! wrench it from him. [*Seizes his wrist.*

Grome. Ah, mistress, wilt thou use me thus? Dost not know me?

N. Methinks I do! Let him not make away with it! [*Still holds* GROME.

Soldier. Yield it, without more words!

[*Two or three soldiers seize* GROME *and take letter from him.*

Grome. Do you not know your comrade?

Sir Thomas. What means this?

Secretary. (*Receiving the letter from a soldier.*) An odd affair! (*Puts on spectacles, looks at letter.*) Hm!

[*Hands it to Sir* THOMAS.

Sir Thomas. (*Looks at it.*) I'll make free in this case. (*Opens and reads letter.*) How got Captain Radclyffe this?

Charlton. (*With an effort.*) I meant not, I own, to appear in this matter—nor know I what that letter contains—but I have been looking after this plot, in the interests of the Parliament.

Mistr. R. Otherwise, playing the spy in this, thy uncle's house?

Sir Thomas. Do you charge Colonel Radclyffe and Lord Lyndore as parties to this plot?

Ch. (*Hesitating.*) I make no charge against them.

Grome. (*Aside.*) A fine tangle we are got into.

Sir Thomas. (*Pointing at* GROME.) Who is this man? Step forward, fellow.

Ch. A corporal in my regiment, Grome by name— left here in trust.

N. In trust!

[GROME *is put forward: his sleeve pushed up by the scuffle.*

Secretary. (*Puts on spectacles.*) Hm—let me look at him. Turn this way. A little more in the light. With your good leave, Sir Thomas. (*Sir* THOMAS *nods.*) Your name is Grome?

Grome. Paul Grome, an't please you.

Secretary. (*Calmly.*) It doth not altogether please me. Methinks, friend, I have been used to know you by other names. At the Winter Assize of the City of London four years ago I knew you by the name of Josiah Peters, *alias* Jack Ludgate. You were convicted of highway robbery and murder, but broke jail and escaped with two other convicts. Afterwards I had tidings of your enlistment under the name of Harry

White in Lord Wilmot's horse, and subsequent desertion from the same, with robbery.

Grome. Sir!—

Secretary. (*Takes off spectacles.*) Give me leave. Since then, you have been in Ireland, and in Holland, under various names. I will confess I looked not to have the pleasure of meeting you to-day.

Grome. (*Stammering.*) Sir, you are a lawyer—Am I the man you saw four years ago?

Secretary. The very same,—only fatter; and with the same scar on your wrist. (*Points:* GROME *hastily covers his wrist.*) Sir Thomas—

[*Speaks low.*

Sir Thomas. Cornet Jebb, you will take charge of him. [GROME *is arrested.*

Ch. I knew nothing of all this. He has deceived me also.

Sir Thomas. Take him away. Colonel Radclyffe, my Lord Lyndore, I must ask you to prepare for your journey.

N. O mother! there is treachery here, and we cannot find it out!—Will you let them be taken to prison?— Sir Thomas Chenery!

Col. R. Hush, Naomi.

[GROME *at door, in custody, is trying to speak: the soldiers forcing him out.*

N. (*Rushing to them.*) Soldiers! let that man stay!

Grome. (*To Sir* THOMAS.) One word!—Will your honour graciously permit one word?—in a contrite and humble spirit!

N. Will you not hear him?

Sir Thomas. Let him speak. (*They bring* GROME *back.*) What would you say?

Cornet Jebb. Speak up, Jack Ludgate!

Grome. Yet why should I, unless his honour will promise me some kindness? Let it be said that mercy and truth have met together.

Sir Thomas. Come, fellow, thy neck is already forfeit. If thou hast aught worth telling, it may serve thee.

Ch. Sir Thomas, will you listen to such a man?

Grome. Relying on your honour's honourable promise, I will briefly say what can be well established by proof. This gentleman (*points to* CHARLTON) has for some three months past been plotting (*coughs*) against his worshipful uncle, Colonel Radclyffe (GROME *bows to Colonel* RADCLYFFE), and against this honourable young nobleman, my Lord Lyndore (GROME *bows to Lord* LYNDORE). He has spread false reports, opened letters, suppressed applications for my lord's exchange, forged papers, and, finally, caused information of treason to the Parliament to be supplied against them.

Ch. Scoundrel!

Sir Thomas (*To* GROME.) Say you so? This in cypher?

Grome. He forged it (*points to* CHARLTON), and I sadly confess that, under his fear, I put it into his lordship's writing-case.

[*Sir* THOMAS *whispers with his Secretary.*

N. (*To her mother.*) I knew not Charlton was so wicked!

Mistr. R. Seeds of good and evil flourish prodigiously under war's fiery climate.

Secretary. (*To* GROME.) You accuse Captain Radclyffe. What motives could he have?

Grome. Verily, first, to get his uncle, whom he loves not, out of his way—along with my lord, whom he loves still less. Then, to make his own throw for fortune,—perhaps a peerage if all went right.

Secretary. How that?

Grome. The Midland Counties Plot is a blind.—The true plot is in Yorkshire and the North. But the true plotters are not these gentlemen, but Master Charlton Radclyffe and certain friends of his.

[*Secretary nods, and whispers to Sir* THOMAS.

Ch. (*Raising himself.*) Rogue and liar!

[*Falls back.*

Sir Thomas. (*To* GROME.) Canst prove this?

Grome. To the last point, sir. I have been on the watch all through. He (*points to* CHARLTON) hath this long while been dealing with the King's party. I can name you many of his complotters. You will get me a pardon, Sir Thomas?

Sir Thomas. (*To Secretary.*) What think you?

[*They whisper.*

Grome. Let him be searched. I shall marvel if you find not proof upon him at this moment.

[*Sir* THOMAS *motions to Cornet* JEBB, *who searches* CHARLTON, *seated in chair, a soldier on each side holding his arms.*

Cornet. A secret pocket—Here's somewhat!

[*Pulls out a small case containing a parchment folded, which he hands to Sir* THOMAS.

Sir Thomas. (*Opens it.*) The King's signature!

Grome. He carried that key to open men's minds to him.

Sir Thomas. What say you to this, Charlton Radclyffe? (CHARLTON *groans and shuts his eyes.*) By and by you may be able to speak. Meanwhile, Colonel Radclyffe, I take upon me to relieve you from arrest (*Secretary nods*), and will add I for one never believed the charges laid against you. Suspicion will melt from your name like breath from your sword-blade.

Col. R. I thank you, Sir Thomas.

[*He joins his wife and daughter.*

Mistr. R. Husband, you are safe!

N. I knew it, father, I knew it!

Sir Thomas. For you, Lord Lyndore, I understand you have suffered no little from a wound taken in saving the life of one of our best officers. (*Bows slightly*

12—2

to Col. RADCLYFFE.) I think you know nothing of this plot.

Lyn. Nothing, sir, upon my honour.

Sir Thomas. How comes Charlton Radclyffe wounded?

Lyn. In no quarrel of my seeking.

Col. R. (*Stepping forward to* CHARLTON.) Speak, sir!

Ch. (*Furiously.*) Would I had struck him dead!

N. (*Shuddering.*) O how should any kin of ours be there!

Sir Thomas. My Lord Lyndore, it is within my power to offer you free pass to your native place, there to live undisturbed, on promise not to move henceforth against the Parliament of England.

> [*All look at* LYNDORE.

Lyn. I most truly thank you, Sir Thomas Chenery; but I cannot accept this offer.

Col. R. Ha!

Sir Thomas. Not accept?

> [*Secretary puts on spectacles and
> looks at Lord* LYNDORE.

N. O mother, why does he refuse?

Mistr. R. Alas!

Sir Thomas. What then would you do, my lord?

Lyn. Ride to Prince Rupert at Bristol.

Sir Thomas. Prince Rupert is not at Bristol.

Lyn. Not there, sir!

Sir Thomas. Bristol is ours.

Col. R. Indeed!   [*General movement.*

Lyn. And Rupert?

Sir Thomas. On his road to Germany perhaps. Pray read your letter, my lord. This is for you. Pardon my freedom of opening it.

> [*Hands him the letter taken from*
> GROME. *Talks to Secretary, who
> also writes on a paper.*

Lyn. (*Takes letter.*) From my trusty old Major

Lucas! (*Steps nearer Col.* RADCLYFFE *and his group, and reads*)—"Strange news to send—Bristol is surrendered—Rupert dismissed by the king and ordered to leave England—his regiment disbanded—your troop all scattered and the men gone home. We heard some lies about you, but believed none. We knew well you would have been with us if you could. The fighting game's up. I shall beat my own sword into a ploughshare, and whistle behind it for better times."—My comrades did not doubt me then!—Radclyffe, thy advice?

Col. R. Your lordship's main duty now is to your own place and people, and you are free to go to them. Else, you are not free to go anywhere.

Mistr. R. Follow my husband's counsel, Lord Lyndore.

Lyn. (*To* NAOMI, *who has fallen into a reverie.*) Do you also thus advise?

N. Your pardon—what, my lord?

Lyn. You heard Sir Thomas Chenery's offer?

N. Yes.

Lyn. Think you I should accept?

N. I do.

Lyn. Sir Thomas Chenery, your pardon,—I thankfully accept the conditions.

Sir Thomas. I am glad to hear it. (*Secretary hands him paper.*) Here is your free pass, my lord. Use it at your convenience. See to the wounded man.

Cornet. He is better. The wound is not grave.

Grome. (*To* CHARLTON.) How feel you, Captain?

Ch. Ready to choke you, villain!

Grome. Alas, sir, you've been so anytime this twelvemonth. (*Fingers his throat.*) Methinks I breathe freer now. They will scarce nurse *you* in this house, Captain.

Sir Thomas. Look well to your prisoners, Cornet Jebb.

Cornet. We shall take them on to our night-quarters,
Sir Thomas.

Sir Thomas. And send them to London as soon as
may be.

Cornet. I shall, sir.

Soldier, to another. To the strong box! and afterwards—(*winks*).

> [CHARLTON *walks out with difficulty,
> guarded; he catches* GROME'S *eye,
> scowls at him and shakes his fist.*

Grome. (*Pointing at Lord* LYNDORE, *who is in
familiar talk with* NAOMI, *and resuming his twang.*)
Verily, Captain, thou hast done *him* a good turn! Yea,
thou hast been exceeding kind unto him!

> [*Exeunt* CHARLTON, GROME, *and some of
> the soldiers. Mistress* RADCLYFFE
> *sends* PRUDENCE *after them;* TOM
> *follows* PRUDENCE *closely, and, in
> going out, glances round to see if he
> is observed, then kisses her neatly,
> not to her discontent.*

Sir Thomas. (*To Col. and Mistress* RADCLYFFE.)
No, I thank you; I must ride further to-night, late as
it is. Ladies, your humble servant! Good-night,
Colonel Radclyffe!—my lord!—

> [*Bows exchanged, Sir* THOMAS *exit deliberately
> (L), soldiers preceding him; attended cere-
> moniously to the door by Col. and Mistress*
> RADCLYFFE. NAOMI *and* LYNDORE *left by
> themselves (R, centre). She is now seated
> in an old carved chair. Her manner grave
> and distant.*

Lyn. Naomi!

N. My lord.

Lyn. You were in haste to dismiss me.

N. You were eager to depart.

Lyn. Are you still in the same mind?

N. More firmly than ever.

Lyn. How mean you?

N. Your road is clear, my lord, and you are bound to go.

Lyn. Not bound to go to-night . . . unless you bid me. If that be your wish . . .—Naomi! dost thou indeed send me away?

N. (*Looks at him, then suddenly stretches out her arms.*) No!   [*He embraces her.*

 [*Col. and Mistress* RADCLYFFE *come from door L. Col.* RADCLYFFE *affectionately holds back his wife, and they stand a moment looking at* NAOMI *and Lord* LYNDORE. NAOMI *sees them.*

N. O dearest parents!

Lyn.   May *I* call you so?

Mistr. R. No better son could bounteous Heaven bestow!

Col. R. Lyndore!—my Naomi!—this plighted troth
Is welcome news to us, who love you both.
And may God grant the future of our land
Be emblem'd by this happy hand in hand.

       [*Joins their hands*

(*Music, introducing* "*Wilt Thou, Summer.*")

Curtain falls slowly.

NOTE.

MAD ROBIN.—This delightful old melody is here, perhaps, published modernly for the first time in its integrity. Chappell's *Popular Music of the Olden Time* is a book with an air of authority, but nevertheless untrustworthy. In vol. ii. p. 512, we find in it: "MAD ROBIN.—This tune is in *The Dancing Master* of 1686 (additional sheet) and all later editions. . . . . I have not succeeded in finding the song of *Mad Robin*, and have therefore taken the first and last stanzas of a ballad contained in a manuscript of the time of James I., now in the possession of Mr. Payne Collier. I have no authority for coupling them with the tune, but prefer these old words to any written expressly to the air in the ballad-operas." The version given is inaccurate, and, indeed, in one place alters the whole character of the air.

I give the exact original music, copied (in the British Museum) from *The Dancing Master*, 7th ed. 1686, in additional tunes at the end. It is not in the 8th ed., 1690, but is in the 9th ed., 1695, page 185.

I have been ignorantly supposed to have taken a fine old Song, tampered with the music, and substituted my own words for the old ones: what I have done is to go back to the oldest known authority for the music, and no old words, so far as I can learn, are in existence. The admirably suitable accompaniment I owe to my friend Mrs. Tom Taylor.

ASHBY MANOR was sent in print to several London Managers, one of whom solicited an interview with the Author, at which he highly praised the Play, regretted that it was not exactly suited to his company, and requested that something else might be submitted to him from the same hand, deprecating strongly, as a detail, the printing of a Play before its appearance on the Stage. Some months later this Manager produced a Play which appeared, not merely to the Author but to others, to be beyond all doubt a kind of clumsy parody of *Ashby Manor*, in time, story, incidents and characters, with senseless melodramatic additions, and an entirely irrelevant fifth act. The Manager, on this being pointed out to him, asserted that he had never read a page of *Ashby Manor*, and scarcely recollected anything about it. His bold enterprise deservedly proved a failure.